Redefine - Text copyright © Emmy Ellis 2024
Cover Art by Emmy Ellis @ studioenp.com © 2024

All Rights Reserved

Redefine is a work of fiction. All characters, places, and events are from the author's imagination. Any resemblance to persons, living or dead, events or places is purely coincidental.

The author respectfully recognises the use of any and all trademarks.

With the exception of quotes used in reviews, this book may not be reproduced or used in whole or in part by any means existing without written permission from the author.

Warning: The unauthorised reproduction or distribution of this copyrighted work is illegal. No part of this book may be scanned, uploaded, or distributed via the Internet or any other means, electronic or print, without the author's written permission.

REDEFINE

Emmy Ellis

Chapter One

Danika Cousins, aka Goddess, didn't know how she was supposed to react to what he'd just said. Had she imagined it? Why would a punter even say that? "There's a lovely little girl in your life who I'll take away if you don't do what I want..." There was only one little girl, but how the hell did he know that? What was he, some kind of stalker bastard?

With her hands above her head, palms against the wall, and her legs spread, he rammed into her from behind, more violently now his words floated around inside her mind. He'd been one of her regulars for a while and hadn't been weird up until now. He grunted then drew away. She turned to watch him pulling his trousers up, his back to her. She'd shower once he was gone, but for now she stood there naked, not even bothering to cover her breasts. What was the point when he'd seen it all before?

"What *did you just say to me?" She had to hear it again.*

He tucked his white shirt in, picked up his navy jacket and shrugged into it. "I think you heard me, didn't you?"

"I thought I did, but I just need to make sure."

He smiled at her, revealing what appeared to be Turkey teeth. "Let me explain first. I am The Organiser, and I organise things. I do what I'm told and don't ask why. I do the job and take the money. You're going to have to do something similar except your reward won't be a wage packet, it'll be your niece remaining safe."

So he had *mentioned Amelia.*

Fear crept up inside her. "What do you mean she'll remain safe? And how do you even know I've got a niece?"

"I watched you to determine what sort of person you are and whether you'll do as you're told. The person who's paying me wants something done, so I found a woman who can do what's needed—you. There's a certain escort agency, and it needs to be closed down pretty quickly. It's encroaching on the person's business."

"Who's the person?"

"Let's call them Purple. If you met them, you'd understand why I chose that name. However, I digress. If you don't get the escort agency shut down inside a week, Purple will send me to collect Amelia."

Danika's heart rate sped up and, nauseated, she lurched to one side with her arm out, patting for a nearby chair. She sat on it, shaking her head, trying to comprehend what he'd said. "I'll do it. Leave Amelia alone."

"That sounded to me as if you were calling the shots. In our relationship, that would be me who dishes out orders. Both of us are having our strings pulled."

"So it appeals to you to even consider stealing a four-year-old child from her mother? What is wrong with you?"

He chuckled and sat on the bed.

She thought about all the times he'd spoken to her during their sessions together. He hadn't once given her the impression he'd chosen her to do some work for this Purple person. She'd thought he was just a regular customer who turned up at this room she rented in a scutty little house. It was safer than being out on the street, although when she'd first started selling her body, she'd had to stand on the corners in all weathers in order to build up her client base. Now she had many of their numbers in her mobile, they found her when they needed her and she directed them here. It wasn't the safest of places, what with other women renting rooms, too, and some of them not even caring who they let in through the front door so long as they could earn some money for their addictions.

Danika wasn't into that. She didn't do this for heroin or cocaine. She did it because sex was the only way she felt loved and wanted. Even if it was strangers giving it to her. She was sure it wouldn't make sense on a therapist's couch, so it was a good job she wasn't going to see one, wasn't it. They were a waste of money, pretending they could see inside your head and fix you.

Nothing could fix her or her sister, Kenzie.

She'd always wondered whether they'd been cursed as soon as they were born. Neither of them had ever had much luck, and it seemed with this man calling himself The Organiser, that luck was just as shitty as it had always been. The thought of him taking Amelia from Kenzie had Danika wanting to throw up. Kenzie wouldn't cope without her child, and she'd certainly never speak to Danika again if she found out Amelia was being used as a pawn; she'd say if Danika didn't do this job for a living, none of this would be happening, and she wouldn't be wrong, would she?

"What do I have to do?" she asked him. "And how come it's today you decided to tell me you're not an average customer?"

"One, you have to put the escort agency out of business, by any means necessary, and I mean any means, and two, I'd learned all I needed to know about you, therefore, I was able to reveal who I am and what I want."

"I know your face. I'd recognise you anywhere. Doesn't that bother you?"

"Who says this beard is real? Who says this hair is? Are these my real teeth? Do I really need glasses? Are my eyes really blue? Is my accent genuine?"

She wanted to punch him. "Okay, point taken."

A chill swept over her, so she stood and collected her silk dressing gown from the back of the door. She had a small wheeled suitcase that she packed all of her work clothes into, and now she wanted to stuff them all away and go home. But she couldn't, she had other customers due this evening and didn't want to let them down. Besides, after this interaction, she needed to feel loved. Mr Potter would help her with that.

She sat and wrapped the dressing gown fronts around her. "How am I supposed to put an escort agency out of business? I don't get it."

"By going to work there. Speaking to the customers. Sending them elsewhere. Quietly ruin their reputation."

"Whose reputation?"

"A married couple. Joseph and Farah Bains."

"But what if there aren't any jobs going?"

"There are."

"But there's no guarantee I'm going to get one."

"Oh, you will." He played with his blond beard. "You have no idea how appealing you are, do you? One look at you and they'll take you immediately. You have an interview tomorrow morning at ten a.m." He took a business card out of his pocket and handed it to her.

She stared down at it.

The Organiser
ACCOMMODATING ALL OF YOUR NEEDS
07986542701

She flipped it over, and he'd written an address, presumably for the escort agency, plus her appointment time. What had he done, contacted them acting as her pimp? It was difficult to think of him as The Organiser when she'd always called him Sebastian. Was it even his name? Did it matter anymore?

She looked up at him and shivered at the way he studied her. Eagle-like. Predatory. "So I just turn up at this place and they're expecting me?"

"That's right."

"Let me double-check: how much time have I got to ruin the business?"

"A couple of weeks."

Hadn't he said 'inside a week' earlier?

Panic flared inside her; if he couldn't get his facts straight now, who was to say he wouldn't fuck about later down the line? She'd never know whether she was coming or going. "What? That might not be enough time. I have to settle in. I have to get to know everybody."

"Okay, then a month, but remember, it's not just you who has to face any consequences if this job doesn't get done. I'm using you to do it, and Purple is using me to do it. I can assure you I won't be taking any blame if you don't manage to fulfil this request — Purple will come after you, not me."

"Why me?"

"I chose you because of how you look and behave. You've got more chance of getting a job there than the other women I sampled."

Sampled. Charming. And was she supposed to feel chuffed at being chosen? "So it's just my bad luck that you happened to pick me?"

"I've been paid fifty thousand to destroy businesses — and I might treat you to dinner after it's all over."

That amount of money had her stomach going over, but more importantly, she had to confirm what he'd just said. "You told me it was an escort agency, and now its businesses plural?"

He laughed and slapped his thigh. "Oh, did I forget to tell you that there's another place called the Orange Lantern, then there's The Angel and Kitchen Street. All of them need to be shut down. Purple would like the customers sent their way."

"But there are places like this house, they're everywhere, and you can't get all of them closed."

"No, but the ones that draw the most attention will. Take the Orange Lantern, for instance. Big house. Out-of-the-way location in a quiet part of the Estate. Hundreds of men go there every week. Every time a new, money-making establishment is discovered, you'll be sent to ruin it."

"But that could take years."

"It could."

"That's not right to expect me to do whatever you want like that. It's not fair."

"Nor would it be fair if you didn't do it and Amelia found herself taken away from her mother. Imagine me having to explain to an innocent little girl that her aunt didn't love her enough to do as she was told."

"I'll do it. I'll do whatever you want, I'm just saying it could take ages."

"Not if you work in two places at once. You could do the escort agency for half of the week and the Orange Lantern for the other. When the agency is taken down you then secure a place at The Angel and so on."

"That's going to be too difficult. There's a massive waiting list for that place."

"Then you'd best get yourself on it now, hadn't you." He stood and smiled. "It's been a pleasure, *although don't take this as a goodbye."* He slid his hand in his pocket and brought out a basic phone. *"It has credit on it and my number. You do not contact me on that unless you have news that the agency has been shut down. If I need to talk to you, I'll find you—remember, I'll always be watching. And think about this: Purple has employed me. I have employed you—granted, without paying you wages—but I could have also employed other people. A kidnapper, for example. Or someone who sits outside Kenzie's house in his car and follows her everywhere."*

Danika thought she might be sick but then calmed. He couldn't have had anyone spying on her sister because Kenzie barely left the house if she could help it. He'd have known that if he'd been watching.

"I get it, okay?" She snatched the phone out of his hand. *"So what, I just live my life doing whatever you want me to do until this Purple person has got everything their own way?"*

"That pretty much sums it up. See you when I see you."

He unlocked the door and stepped out onto the landing, grinning as he shut her inside. She closed her burning eyes and shivered. What were the odds that she'd been chosen to do this out of hundreds of sex workers? The idea that he'd had an agenda for her from the start gave her the creeps. Even more so that he knew about Kenzie and Amelia. Was *there a man sitting outside their house right now in a car?*

She turned to reach for her handbag on the sideboard to take her phone out, but the cheap one in her hand bleeped. She stared down at the preview message and opened it fully.

THE ORGANISER: I FORGOT TO SAY... IF YOU TELL THE BROTHERS, YOU'RE DEAD. IF YOU TELL THE POLICE, YOU'RE DEAD. IF YOU DO ANYTHING OTHER THAN WHAT I TELL YOU, YOU'RE DEAD. [SMILE EMOJI]

She wanted to throw the phone but switched it off and put it in her handbag. She found her personal mobile and quickly brought up Kenzie's name. How was she supposed to tell her sister that her daughter might be kidnapped? How could she stop Kenzie from going to The Brothers or the police with that information? The truth was, she couldn't. Kenzie wasn't the type to take this shit sitting down. She wouldn't care that Danika's life was in danger. She had a daughter to protect and she'd do whatever it took to keep her safe, even if that meant her own sister got killed in the process.

That's what was going to happen, wasn't it? The Organiser's text had said as much. If she didn't get on with it, she was dead.

The burner phone trilled out again.

THE ORGANISER: OH, AND IF YOU MESSAGE KENZIE, YOU'RE DEAD. [LOVE HEART EMOJI]

Danika glanced around the room in panic. Had he put one of those tiny cameras in here? Was he watching her? If not, how did he know she was about to text Kenzie? Or was it just a coincidence? That was two messages he'd sent, telling her things he maybe should have mentioned before he'd left the room. Did that mean he wasn't as organised as his name had led her to believe? Or had it been on purpose, a little reminder that he could text her and say scary things whenever he liked?

What was it he'd said, though? That if he needed to contact her, he'd find her. That meant he wouldn't message her. In that case, she'd switch the burner off and stick it in a shoebox in her wardrobe at home. If he wasn't going to use it to get hold of her, what was the point in having it?

Maybe it has a tracker on it.

She wanted to respond to him and tell him to fuck off but didn't have the balls. With all avenues of help blocked off, she had no choice but to do what he wanted. And it wouldn't be so bad, would it? A few whispers in the punters' ears and they'd soon stop going to the escort agency. But there were probably thousands of people on the books, so how was she supposed to get to them all? She'd have to think of another way to bring the business down.

She quickly had a shower and forced her mind onto the next customer. There was plenty of time to frighten herself stupid about what had just happened later. Losing herself in sex with a near stranger would help her forget, just for a moment, that she was once again in a situation she didn't want to be in.

Chapter Two

The Organiser had been holding his temper for quite some time, but now he needed to speak to Danika before he lost the plot completely. What the hell had she been playing at? He'd discovered she'd been involved with the twins, and if he found out she'd gone running to them about *him*... But what could he do? They might be watching him now. He'd have to be careful.

She'd been dropped off by a man in a red car. He'd switched his usual blond beard and wig to brown for this interaction. He was aware she was friendly with her next-door neighbour, a woman called Oaklynn, and he wasn't sure whether Danika had the balls to confide in her about what was going on. She may have described him to the woman, so to cover his arse, he'd gone for the dark-haired look and brown eyes. His car had fake plates, so he wasn't bothered about those, and there were thousands of white Mokkas around.

He left his car and walked up her garden path, annoyed she'd drawn all the curtains when usually they were open and he could see inside plain as day. She had a front door with clear glass in it, which was also covered. He knocked on it, knowing she was in, unless she'd nipped to Oaklynn's via the back garden.

A creak sounded from above, and he looked up. She'd opened a bedroom window and, head poking out, stared down at him. Her face paled, as it well might, and without saying a word, she closed the window. He waited patiently for her to draw the curtain across on the front door and let him in. He stepped inside, the scent of her perfume, now familiar, wrapping around him. He wished he'd met her in other circumstances. At one point, he'd talked himself out of using her, wanting to keep her as his lady of the night instead, but she was the classiest woman he'd found, one who could pull off being an escort at the agency, so sadly, despite his budding feelings for her, he'd had to put them aside.

He had to be nasty to her now in order to stand being in her presence. If he let himself feel anything sweet towards her, this could go tits up. He might tell her he was sorry. He might let her off the hook.

No, Purple will be cruel to me if I don't pull this off.

He walked off into her kitchen at the back without being invited to do so. He had the upper hand here and always would in their relationship—a far cry from any other relationship going on in his life. He had no control there. He settled himself at the dining table and drummed his fingertips on top, the sound deadened by the leather of his gloves. He wasn't stupid enough to enter this house and leave any prints.

She looked like she'd been crying. A lot. She'd not long sent him a message to say that Farah and Joseph were out of the loop, and he'd responded that her next job was to destroy Widow from the Orange Lantern and for her not to contact him again until she'd done it. That didn't mean *he* couldn't contact *her*. She was used to him popping up at different times now with his little messages and taunts and threats.

"Have you been blubbing?" he asked.

"Isn't it obvious?"

"Well, yes, that's why I asked, to make a point and show you I noticed. I've come to find out what 'out of the loop' means."

"They're dead. The twins killed them."

Shock almost pitched him forward and up to his feet, but he had to remain calm, as if murder was an everyday topic of conversation for him. He'd told her to get the job done by any means necessary, and she had.

Jesus Christ. Now let her know you were watching her. "So *that* was what you were doing with them."

She frowned. "Why the hell else do you think I'd be involved with them? You put me in an impossible situation. You asked me to destroy the escort agency and the sex warehouse, yet there was no way I could do it without taking the route I just have. I told the twins that Joseph and Farah were bullying me, and they took exception to that. They put me in a safe house overnight while they rounded them up and got rid of them—one of their men brought me home, so if you were spying, that was him in the red car. I don't know where the bodies are and I don't care. All I'm bothered about is that I've done what you asked and now you want me to go after Widow—but shouldn't that be ruining the Orange Lantern?"

"Yes, that's what I meant." God, he wasn't as good at this lark as he'd hoped. He didn't want another person's death on his conscience, so Widow had to remain alive.

He needed to take a moment to process Danika's resourcefulness. He hadn't expected her to have thought outside the box *that* much. She'd committed murder without even getting her hands dirty, and he admired her for that. Yes, she was desperate because she had a ticking clock going against her, but so did he. The escort agency and the sex warehouse would no longer operate because the owners had no family to take over, which was a great weight off his mind.

Purple had been getting impatient of late because he hadn't fulfilled the requirements quickly enough.

Thankfully, he'd taken great pleasure in letting Purple know that Farah and Joseph had been taken care of, but Purple had wanted to know what that meant, hence why The Organiser was here. He didn't have to ask the question about The Brothers now because Danika had already answered it. The issue he *did* have was how cosy she'd got with them.

"What's the score regarding the twins?"

"I'm going to have to be careful. Maybe they're going to be watching me now to see if I act dodgy. I'm going to have to bring the Lantern down behind the scenes even more than I would've done previously."

"Why would they want to watch you?"

"I don't know. I've just got a feeling they will."

He didn't believe her. She was just saying that to buy herself more time. "When you started at the Lantern, someone else ran it, but now The Brothers do. If you thought ruining the escort agency and the warehouse was difficult, the Lantern is going to be even more so."

"Not really, because the twins are barely there. It's Widow I need to worry about. I would have said Precious, too, but she no longer works there."

That was interesting. "Why is that when she's been there from the start?"

"I don't know. I didn't think I should be asking any questions, considering I'm about to ruin their business."

He didn't like her tone. "Watch how you speak to me."

"D'you know what? I am so *tired* of this. I've been dancing to your tune for ages, yet when I ask you for one simple little picture, you can't show it to me. Where's that little girl you've stolen from my sister? Where the fuck have you put her?"

He stood, annoyance surging through his body. "Like I've just said, watch how you speak to me. *I'm* the one who can end that girl's life. *I'm* the one who can snap her neck like a twig. Until you've either given me fifty thousand pounds so I can return the payment to Purple to get out of this fucking job, or you destroy the Lantern, The Angel, and Kitchen Street, only then will the girl be returned. You know the stakes. I've told you how it is. I shouldn't have to keep repeating myself. I thought I'd made it pretty clear."

"Can't you at least tell me who looks after her when you're not there?"

"She's in good hands, that's all you need to know."

"I have twenty grand," she said. "The twins gave it to me as compensation for putting up with Farah and Joseph. Even if I get extra tips and clients at the Lantern, I'm never going to make thirty up in such a short space of time."

"It took you long enough to do the first job with Joseph and Farah, so if that's anything to go by, you'll probably have the fifty saved way before you get the jobs done."

She gave him a filthy look. "Please leave, I need to get ready. I've got to pop to my sister's house to make sure she's okay."

"From what I can gather, she's fine."

"So you've got spies in her street, even though the police are there?"

"I've got spies everywhere." He didn't, but it wouldn't hurt her to think that. "I was seen taking the child. I've been contemplating shutting up the woman who told the police."

"She's got a son. Just leave her alone. Let's concentrate on what we need to do instead of adding more things to the mix. I'm actually at the point where I'm worried I'm going to have a breakdown. If you want me to continue doing this, then I need as little stress as possible."

He could understand that. He was under a lot of stress himself. "How are you going to ruin the Lantern?"

"By telling lies about the other women having sexually transmitted diseases. It's all I can think of doing."

"But they're all tested regularly, so will the punters believe that?"

"Would you take the chance if you'd stuck your dick inside a sex worker, despite wearing a condom, if someone told you they were riddled with a disease?"

He had to give it to her, it was a good plan but not perfect. "But what if Widow gets wind of the rumours and one of the punters tells her it was you who was telling tales? She could then tell The Brothers, and I can't see them treating you very nicely, can you? Not after what they've just done for you—they'll see it as a massive betrayal."

"I wasn't going to tell them to their faces, I was going to leave notes in their coat pockets. They have to hang them up in the hallway before they're allowed upstairs with the women—safety reasons, they could have brought a knife in, that sort of thing. I'll follow each man down and help them get their coats on, slipping a note in while I'm at it. It'll be easy once Cameron's not there."

"Who's Cameron?"

"He's a bodyguard the twins brought in when they thought I might be in danger from Farah and Joseph. Now they're dead, I doubt very much Cameron will be staying, unless George and Greg decide it's a good idea to have a guard there all the time. But I can still slip things into their pockets. I can still help them into their coats, even if there's someone standing at the bottom of the stairs. As far as Widow's concerned, it could be any of the women who leaked the lies."

"Wouldn't they look at you because you're one of the last ones to start work there? They didn't have any problems and then you come along and there's rumours about diseases."

"I think I've endeared myself to the twins enough that they wouldn't listen anyway."

"You'd better hope that's true. You'll need to add my burner number to the bottom of the notes and say that's the one to call for a new sex venue. Have you put your name on the waiting list at The Angel yet?"

"I haven't had time. I've had a man on my back forcing me to do things I don't want to do, plus my niece has been abducted, so I've been a little bit busy."

He fancied she'd got an attitude on her since he last seen her. Maybe having the twins helping her had given her a sense of self-importance. "How did you get along with The Brothers? You said you endeared yourself to them... Do I need to worry?"

"No. They're scary, they're very thorough, they get the job done, and they swallowed my sob story. As I was frightened of them, and of you in case you thought I'd grassed you up to them, I wasn't in the best place mentally to particularly get to know them."

"So you haven't come out of this being their friend?"

"I'm just a resident. They helped, nothing more. They gave me compensation, something they do with lots of people, and that's the end of it."

"What would you say if they asked you to do a job for them which meant you'd get another twenty grand?"

"It depends what it is, and it's not likely to happen anyway, is it."

"What if it was enough to make the complete fifty?"

"Then I'd want you to take me to Purple so I can hand the money over myself. Call me silly, but I don't trust you." Her sarcasm seemed so loud. "You could be making it up that you can get out of the job by paying Purple back, then keep the cash for yourself. I'm sorry, but I'm done with being treated as though I'm stupid."

"I admire you for being so candid. Or perhaps that's silly for thinking you can speak to me that way when I have your four-year-old niece in captivity. Like I said, I could snap her neck and not even blink."

"How did you even get into this business?"

"The dark web. We've all got the same name: The Organiser. There are loads of us all around the country. The jobs are placed online, along with the fee people are prepared to pay, and The

Organisers bid for it. I have to say, I wish I'd lost my bid for this job. Purple is the most impatient client, despite me telling them the destruction of people's businesses can take months."

She eyed him funny. "How do I know you're not just making that up? How do I know Purple even exists?"

"That's the beauty of it, you don't. You do as you're told or, well, you know what will happen." He stood. "I'll let myself out." He strode to the door and then stopped to say over his shoulder, "I'd find somewhere safe to put that twenty grand if I were you because I can't imagine they gave it to you via bank transfer. Some people have no shame in breaking into houses and stealing what isn't theirs."

Her sharp intake of breath told him all he needed to know: she'd realised her mistake in mentioning the compensation money. Who would she give it to? Would it be Oaklynn next door? Or was she friendlier with the twins than she'd led him to believe and she'd take it to them? If she had any sense, the safest place would be Kenzie because the police were still there. But then would she want to risk the house being searched again and the money being discovered?

No, he doubted it.

He whistled and got in his car, checking his appearance in the rearview mirror. Taking out a Chapstick and using it to smooth down his eyebrows, he deemed himself presentable enough to go to the Noodle for his lunch. You never know, he might pick up some snippets of conversation while he was there, seeing as the twins owned the gaff.

Chapter Three

Danika wished she didn't have to be here. It was all The Organiser's fault, and she was sick to death of doing whatever he said. She teetered on the verge of telling the twins everything, right down to the fact that one of their four-year-old residents had been kidnapped and it had barely been in the news. If she started from the beginning and explained how she'd been coerced into doing certain things, then she was sure they'd understand, the same as they had when she'd asked them for help regarding Farah and Joseph. But what they might not understand was she hadn't told them everything at the same time, even though a little girl was God knew where.

The twenty grand seemed to burn a hole in her bag. She wasn't going to leave it at Kenzie's, but it was safer to have it with her. She knocked on Kenzie's door, expecting the family liaison officer, Ellie, to open up and let her in. But Kenzie stood there, bedraggled and exhausted-looking. The police had asked the doctor to give her a sedative so she could actually get some sleep because she'd been driving herself mad as to where her daughter was. Danika knew damn well what had happened, but she couldn't say anything. If she admitted to the police what had gone on, she'd likely be seen as an accomplice to the kidnap. At least if she told The Brothers, she'd have a better chance of them believing her.

Kenzie wandered away and headed towards the kitchen at the end of the hallway. Danika looked back at the street to check for Ellie's red car, but it wasn't there. Had Kenzie sent her away? Had Ellie's questions become too intrusive? Or maybe her presence had been too much, seeing as Kenzie preferred to keep to herself. She wasn't a mixer and didn't have any friends. Her whole life had been her daughter, Amelia, although a few days ago you wouldn't have believed she even cared about the child. The house had been a shit state, Amelia grubby, her hair a mess. It was only now she was gone that Kenzie seemed to have realised she needed to buck up and look after her properly.

Danika closed the door and slipped the chain on, mindful The Organiser could send someone around here to hurt her sister. She hadn't had the conversation with her yet as to why she wanted Kenzie to ensure she was locked in, but now that the police weren't staying here, she felt it was time.

She entered the kitchen and glanced at Kenzie, who sat at the dining table.

"I heard you put the chain on again," Kenzie grumbled. "Why do you keep doing that?"

"Because someone got in this house and took your child and they could come back and take you. I can't lose you both." Yes, she'd been blunt, but she always had to be with Kenzie. If you beat around the bush, she tended to ignore you. "Indulge me and lock yourself in whenever you're alone." She filled the kettle and flipped the switch. "Where's Ellie?"

"I told her I needed a break. She was nice enough and everything, but God, it's doing my head in having someone here all the time."

"Is that a hint for me to piss off?"

Kenzie chuffed out a laugh. "No. I wouldn't hint with you, I'd just outright say so."

Danika smiled and took cups out of the dishwasher, adding instant coffee and sweeteners. While the kettle boiled, she did a bit of cleaning. Ellie had been really good in keeping on top of everything since she'd been here. Maybe now Kenzie had seen how nice her house could look while it was clean and tidy, it might give her the impetus to keep it up herself, although to be fair, with her daughter being abducted it was probably the last thing on her mind.

Danika made the coffee and took the cups over to the table. She sat and sighed, desperately wanting to open up and tell Kenzie why Amelia had been taken. But like she'd thought several times, Kenzie was the type to go straight to the police with whatever Danika said, and who could blame her? She just wanted her child back.

"Have you had any dinner?" she asked instead.

Kenzie shook her head. Danika got her phone out and browsed the Chinese menu, suffering a sense of déjà vu. This wasn't the first time she'd fed her sister. Kenzie hadn't exactly got her shit together. Their childhood had ruined them both, but only one of them had managed to carve a decent life out for themselves. Kenzie had found herself unable to bear the weight of what had happened to them, and depression had claimed her.

Danika hated their father for what he'd done. When all this was over with The Organiser, she was going to approach the twins about killing Matthew Cousins. Maybe even their mother, too, for her part in it all.

So she didn't dwell on it, she concentrated on ordering, not asking Kenzie what she wanted because she always had the same thing: sweet and sour pork balls and chips. It was like a punch to the gut that she hadn't added chicken fried rice to the list, Amelia's favourite.

"Who would want my little girl?" Kenzie asked.

It was something they'd spoken about a few times now. Kenzie was a loner, and lately, she didn't leave the house very often. If this had been a genuine abduction, where Danika hadn't known the child was going to be taken, she would be so confused as to why Amelia had been whisked away. She didn't even go to school yet, so a perv couldn't have been watching her in the playground.

"I don't know," Danika said. "But I promise we'll get her back."

"How can you promise? It's not the sort of thing you can guarantee. I heard Ellie talking to that McFarlane copper. They think she might have been stolen to sell on for adoption or some paedo has got her. I'd woken up and I was standing at the top of the stairs and heard them. I didn't let them know I was there, I went into the bathroom instead. What if it wasn't them speculating and they're right? What if she's with a new family now and she likes them better than me? If they're genuine people who just want a child, they're going to give her everything she could ever want, aren't they? All the things I can't give her. She won't want to come home to this shithole." She sighed. "At least she won't grow up a basket case if I'm not her mother. Will she forget me? Or will she remember who I am and try to find me when she's older? And as for it being a paedo... Fucking hell, I can't stop thinking about it."

"Did the doctor leave you enough sedatives for tonight?"

"Ellie's going to bring a tablet round later. I don't suppose they can trust me with having more than one at a time." Kenzie laughed. "You know, they might think I'll top myself, and I've been bloody tempted, I can tell you."

"You can't do that. Amelia will come home. And when she does, what do I tell her if you're not here?"

"You tell her you'll be her new mummy."

Danika schooled her features so they didn't give her away. She had to believe The Organiser had kept Amelia safe and she'd be home at some point, because she didn't want the responsibility of a child if Kenzie decided she could no longer continue living.

"You listen to me," Danika said. "We'll never give up hope. She *will* be home. We just have to try and remain sane while we wait. The police will find her eventually, they've got to."

"But there's all those other kiddies who've gone missing. They don't find them, and if they do, bones have been dug up somewhere. It hasn't even been in the newspapers, so nobody else is looking for her, they don't know she's missing. Ellie said that's because they want to keep it low profile so the abductor's not aware of what they're doing. She reckons if it fills newspapers, the police would have to give updates. At least this way they can look for her quietly, but my God, even though I understand their methods, I don't like it. I want to shout to everybody that my daughter's gone. I want to see her face on the telly and Facebook."

This was the most genuine Danika had seen Kenzie since Amelia had gone missing. Maybe it was finally sinking in now. Maybe at first she'd convinced herself she must be imagining it, that this wasn't really happening and it was a dream. It had probably been too surreal, all those coppers pouring into the house, the neighbours out the front trying to find a little girl who they thought had just wandered out of her house after she'd woken up, disorientated.

Danika reached out and squeezed Kenzie's hand. "Do you want me to stay here tonight?"

"No. I've got a feeling when I take my tablet that Ellie will come and sleep over anyway, so I'll be all right."

They drank their coffee, then the Chinese arrived and Danika dished it up. She had ordered extra in case Kenzie got hungry later. They ate in companionable silence, although a million words were backed up behind Danika's lips, waiting to explain. To tell her sister she was sorry to have put her through this but she'd had no choice.

They watched a film through the afternoon, and then Danika had to get to work. On one hand, she hated leaving Kenzie, but on the other, she couldn't wait to get out of the house. She walked two streets away to the bus stop and hopped on board, already looking forward to losing herself in the punters. She'd ask Widow if she could pop her compensation money in the safe, and tomorrow, she'd type out the notes about the sexual diseases and add The Organiser's phone number.

But she might not put the cards in any pockets.

Chapter Four

Danika had been calling herself Goddess at work for a long time now, but for the first time, she didn't feel anything like her name. She wasn't some all-powerful being—a disguise she stepped into every day—but a pawn in a nasty little game. She stood outside the building where the escort agency was situated and worried about what she was supposed to say when she went inside. She was going to look stupid if they mentioned something she was unaware of, like who'd organised her interview.

She'd barely slept last night and had to cover the bags under eyes with copious amounts of concealer. She'd phoned Kenzie for a chat before bed, asking casual questions so she knew that everything was okay. It felt wicked to know Amelia might be kidnapped at some point and that she couldn't say anything about it. Honestly, Kenzie would just go straight to the police and fuck everything up. Danika would likely do the same in her position.

She glanced around the street at the other glass-fronted, high-rise buildings that appeared to be offices. Each one had a car park at the front. Was The Organiser watching her from his vehicle? Was he taking pictures for Purple to prove she was doing as she was told? Did Purple even exist, or were they just made up to make everything sound scarier? She sensed eyes on her, but there were hundreds of windows on either side of the street and anyone could be staring at her from their desks. There had to be CCTV here, too.

She turned back to the escort agency building. A woman dressed in elegant clothing came out, a waft of perfume trailing in her wake along with a red silk scarf flapping in the breeze. Danika guessed she worked for the agency, considering she looked so well put together, or maybe everyone who worked inside looked like that. Danika had made sure she'd dressed in a nice suit, not any of her usual clothing. She'd guessed this place was a bit more top-end than the room she rented in the scutty house. The last thing Mr and Mrs Bains would expect was for her to walk in wearing a mini skirt and red high heels, they'd want someone classy.

She checked her phone. Five minutes to ten. Better that she was a little early. She pushed the door and stepped inside a small square foyer, automatic double doors ahead, gliding apart and allow her in. She went through into a large reception area with sofas and lots of pink and peach mood lighting, tall fake plants, and a bookshelf filled with magazines.

A woman of about twenty sat behind a curved wooden desk and smiled at her. "Can I help you?"

Danika nodded. "I'm here for a ten o'clock appointment."

"Which company is that with, please?"

Shit. She didn't really want to say it out loud but supposed if the woman worked here and dealt with all the businesses, she was used to people coming about the escort agency. Danika took a deep breath and gave her the name.

"Ah, right. Yes. If you go down that corridor there and turn left, you'll see another reception there."

"Thank you."

Danika walked that way, her heels clip-clopping on the shiny marble floor. It must cost a fortune to rent offices here. Even the air smelled expensive. She rounded the corner, confronted with another curved desk, this time a blonde woman sitting behind it, her almost-black lipstick stark against her pale face.

"Hello, I'm Danika Cousins, and I'm here for a ten o'clock appointment."

The receptionist glanced at her computer screen. "Second door on the left. They're expecting you."

For some reason, Danika thought she'd be escorted, but clearly not. She floundered. "Do I just tap on the door or...?"

"Yes, just knock."

Danika wanted to run and go home, but a quick thought of Amelia flashed through her mind and propelled her towards the door. She knocked and waited, her chest tight, her heart beating too fast.

"Come in," someone said on the other side. A man.

She opened the door and poked her head round, smiling, putting on her work persona. The couple sat at a long and shiny board-meeting table, water glasses in front of them as well as laptops. Opposite was an empty glass. She estimated that standing, Mr Bains would be around six feet; black, broad, and good-looking. Assuming the woman was his wife, Danika idly wondered whether she struggled to tame her unruly ginger hair.

"Danika Cousins?" Mr Bains asked.

"Yes, that's me."

"Come and take a seat." He was all smiles and gestured to the chair opposite.

Danika walked towards it, scrutinised by Mrs Bains who was probably assessing every aspect of Danika's appearance and behaviour. Nervous that she'd come across as unsuitable for the job, Danika sat and smiled. Mr Bains poured sparkling water from a large glass bottle.

"Thank you." She sipped as her mouth had gone dry.

"Tell us how you heard about the job," he asked.

She was going to have to tell the truth, or as close to it as she dared to get. "It was through one of my customers actually. I only know him as Sebastian, and without a surname, I don't suppose that's any help to you. He said I'd love it here. I expect he's a customer?"

"Do you know anything about our company?" Mr Bains steepled his fingers.

"Only that it's a high-class escort agency." She'd *learned as much online last night, legitimate dating for the rich, and if sex was on the table afterwards, there had been no mention of it on the internet.*

Mrs Bains studied her intently. "And you're high-class, are you?"

Danika blushed. "Probably not, no, but I can pretend to be."

Mrs Bains smiled. "Good answer. Are you aware that we don't allow our employees to have sexual contact with our agency customers?"

"I assumed as much, yes."

Mrs Bains twirled a pen between her fingers. "Are you currently working in the side of the industry where you take money for sex?"

"Yes." Danika felt dirty. Somehow, the woman had reduced her to nothing but a filthy slag with those few words. That was the shame Danika always felt when she was questioned about her work choices by people who had a superior air about them.

"And are you prepared to give that up and only work for us?"

"It depends how much you pay me. If my wage here would cover everything I need to earn, then yes, I can give it up. If not, then I'm not the right person for you."

Mrs Bains cocked her head. "Would you consider, later down the line, another sexual interaction job were it to be presented to you by myself or my husband?"

Bloody hell, does she mean me having sex with them?

"It would depend what that was." For now, she'd play along in order to get the job. And in all honesty, she'd likely jump at the chance for sexual interaction in the future, but of course, she could stand on a street corner or go to a pub and pick someone up for that kind of thing.

"It isn't here, you understand," Mr Bains said. "There is absolutely no sex while working for this escort agency. However, we do have another venture in the pipeline and have been asking all of our employees whether they would be prepared to work there some evenings. We won't go into details today because you're here for the position as an escort."

They chatted for a while longer, and at the mention of her wages, per night, she had to stop herself from screeching in shock. A thousand pounds for every evening up until midnight and another thousand afterwards for unsociable hours. It was more than she'd ever dreamed of earning, and all just to go out for dinner with rich men who needed to pretend they had a girlfriend.

"I think you'll fit in well here." Mr Bains smiled. *"How soon can you start?"*

She really ought to say tonight, but unless The Organiser knew these two, he wouldn't be aware of when her first shift would be until she told him. "Monday?"

"Make it Friday and we have a deal." Mrs Bains smiled, but it didn't reach her eyes. *"Fridays and Saturdays are the busiest, and we could do with you on board as soon as possible."*

Danika nodded. That would be okay. She could message her current clients and let them know she was shutting her doors—or legs—for the time being and if they wanted to see her, it would have to be before close of business on Thursday. That was two days to squeeze in a lot of men.

Mr and Mrs Bains discussed the terms of her employment and went through a contract. She could leave at any time, without notice, but had to fulfil her last client if she had been booked. She had to sign an NDA with every customer, as well as with the agency. It all seemed above board, and even if it wasn't, it didn't matter. She had to be here. She had to ruin the business, then she could move on to the Orange Lantern.

She left the building, wishing she'd got the job on her own terms, that she'd even heard the job was available before The Organiser had told her about it. Despite being forced into this, maybe she should use it to her advantage. She could save a lot of cash towards the fifty grand for Purple, plus try to get herself out of the mindset of having sex to feel loved. Going out for dinner with men instead would perhaps stop her from thinking only having a dick inside her made her worthy of love.

If it hadn't have been for the abuse in her childhood, she wouldn't even think that way.

"Daddy will love you best if you suck his cock…"

"You'll be Daddy's favourite girl if you…"

She'd done so many things a little one should never do, and he'd told her she was his best girl until she'd found out she wasn't. Turned out Kenzie was his best girl, too, and he'd told them both to keep his attentions a secret from the other. It wasn't until Danika had caught them in a compromising position that her world had come crashing down.

Together, they'd tried to come to terms with how they'd been manipulated and why they'd even felt the need to be the best girl in the first place—realising their father had groomed them into thinking that's what they'd needed. Their sibling rivalry meant he'd been able to use it against them in order to get what he wanted. He'd forever broken them, as had their mother, who'd told them to stop telling tales when they'd gone to her for help. They only had each other in the end. Leaving home as soon as they could and setting up in a cheap bedsit together, they hadn't gone back, hadn't seen either parent.

They'd gone their separate ways, renting houses, when they'd got themselves in better financial situations. While Danika turned to strange men and got paid for it, Kenzie picked blokes up in pubs and did it for free, but the need was the same—to be loved. Kenzie didn't know who Amelia's father was, and she said it didn't matter, she had enough love for both parents.

Danika blinked away tears and walked in the direction of the Tube. She had to wait for information regarding her first client, what she needed to wear, where the date was, and what time she had to arrive, all via messages. A picture of the man would be sent so she knew who to approach. Some nights a car might be sent for her, and again, she'd be informed of that prior to the date.

She was still unsure how she'd be able to ruin the business. Surely the men who had enough money to pay for an escort wouldn't be the type to listen to her telling them to go elsewhere. And where *was it? The Organiser hadn't said. What kind of establishment did Purple run? Was it the same as the escort agency or better? If it was better, why did Purple want the kind of punters who'd use the Orange Lantern, The Angel, and Kitchen Street? They wouldn't be able to afford the fees. It didn't make sense, but she supposed it didn't have to. She'd been given a task and somehow had to make it happen.*

Chapter Five

The Organiser stared at his computer screen. Purple had made contact *again*, impatient that the Lantern hadn't been brought to its knees yet. *How* many times had The Organiser explained what was going on? Purple couldn't be pacified and was the type to want what they wanted now, no excuses. To be fair, they had waited a good while for the agency and sex warehouse to be removed from the equation, but as The Organiser had explained, it had been a tricky one.

So was the conversation afterwards.

THE ORGANISER: THE SUBJECTS IN QUESTION ARE NO LONGER IN THE LOOP.

CLIENT: WHAT DOES THAT EVEN MEAN?

The Organiser hadn't responded; he hadn't told Purple he was using Danika to do the dirty work. Maybe he should come clean and say he'd used a third party, that he'd been resourceful, but would that create more issues? Yes, because he'd signed an NDA to say everything he was doing was confidential.

He read the latest message.

CLIENT: HAVE YOU SPREAD THE RUMOURS YET?

THE ORGANISER: I ONLY TOLD YOU ABOUT THAT IDEA AN HOUR AGO, GIVE ME A CHANCE!

CLIENT: YOU SAID YOU'D OBTAINED ALL OF THEIR PHONE NUMBERS, SO WHY HAVEN'T YOU SENT THE TEXTS? WHAT'S THE HOLDUP?

That was the problem with lying—or maybe that should be called bragging in this case. He'd made out he'd tapped into the Lantern's computer database and stolen the clients' phone numbers, bigging himself up so he looked good. He was desperate for recognition, for Purple to see he was someone who could be trusted.

He left it three minutes before he answered.

THE ORGANISER: I'VE JUST SENT THEM NOW. LET'S SEE HOW QUICKLY THE LANTERN CLOSES DOWN. IN THE MEANTIME, I'LL LOOK INTO HACKING THE ANGEL'S DATABASE AND DO THE SAME THERE.

CLIENT: BUT THE TWINS ARE INVOLVED WITH THAT PLACE WITH DEBBIE, SO THERE'S LIKELY A STRONG FIREWALL.

THE ORGANISER: THEY OWN THE LANTERN, AND THAT DIDN'T STOP ME…

CLIENT: THAT DOESN'T ADD UP. THEY'RE USUALLY SO DILIGENT. HAVE YOU BEEN TELLING ME THE TRUTH? HAVE YOU REALLY HACKED INTO ANYTHING?

His stomach muscles bunched. Why did he always have to make himself out to be better than he was? Why couldn't he just state that things were in hand and leave it at that? It was the expectations of his father that had done it: *"Always got to be the best, son."* Those kinds of words stuck with you right into adulthood.

He closed his computer down, his mind filling up. Purple ran a decent sex racket, but it was women on the streets or in doss houses, nothing like the agency. They hoped that by getting rival places shut down it would mean all the business would go their way, but it was flawed. Some men had standards, and they weren't prepared to pick up druggie skanks off corners just to get their end away. The agency et cetera were miles above Purple's business in class, and those punters would probably go to another Estate to find a decent tart once it was clear all that was left were the dregs.

Purple had ideas of grandeur they couldn't deliver. It was like comparing a scabby burger van on the side of the road to a five-star restaurant.

The Organiser thought about the main thing bugging him: having to pay back the fifty grand he'd already been paid to do the job. Unfortunately, it had been in the contract he'd signed. If the jobs weren't completed, the payment had to be returned, regardless of the amount of work The Organiser had already done. He should have queried it at the time but he'd been in a bit of gambling debt and needed to sort that out.

"Always read the small print, son…"

But what if he didn't pay it? The only thing stopping him from sticking to the contract he'd signed was his morals—laughable, but honestly, he had a thing about sticking to his word: *"If you do that, it makes you a man, kid."* Maybe he could stuff his conscience to one side on this occasion. What if he just screwed it and gave Purple the silent treatment? Or better yet, anonymously tipped The Brothers off that they had a pimp in their midst desperate to take over the sex industry in the East End. Danika could go off into the sunset and do her own thing, he'd give Amelia back, and Purple would get a severe kicking from the twins.

Hmm.

The Organiser switched from his computer to his laptop and selected the camera for the loft. The floor had been boarded, the whole area renovated, although he'd yet to have a dormer window fitted. He had proper stairs going up to it, the extra living space originally intended to be his bedroom. But for now, a little girl sat on the rug and played with a Barbie he'd bought for her. She was too doped up to scream; he'd given her just enough so she could function but not be properly coherent. Her head would feel woolly, and each thought would take a few seconds to formulate, a delayed reaction.

He'd lied to Danika. The child wasn't in safe hands when he wasn't there—she was alone. He couldn't risk employing someone to babysit, and anyway, there was no one he trusted, no one he could manipulate and threaten in time. He hadn't intended to abduct Amelia, but the pressure from Purple had pushed him to warn Danika that if she didn't pull her finger out, things were going to change. And now look. She understood he was a man of his word.

He'd taken his suit off when he'd come home, changing into his favourite grey tracksuit bottoms and matching hoodie. It was amazing what a good outfit did for a person, because now he had no wig and beard on and he'd removed his fake veneers, he could be perceived as a lout.

During his time as The Organiser, he'd become many different people, many different types. He made people believe what he presented to them. Danika thought he was a professional businessman, and he was, but to look at him without his disguise on, no. She wouldn't glance twice at him in the street. She wouldn't know he was The Organiser, which was why it had been easy to follow her without her realising it. Despite him warning her that his hair and beard might not really be his, she'd still be looking for him as the put-together man she knew.

He collected some food and went up to the loft and unlocked the door, stepping inside. Amelia slowly turned her head towards him and, seeing it was him, she returned her attention to the doll, not an ounce of fear in her. He closed the door, locking it, taking the tray of food and drink to her. He placed it on the floor and sat with her cross-legged, waiting for her to reach out and take the sandwich.

She didn't.

Surely she couldn't know the food was drugged. She wasn't old enough to even understand what drugs were. But maybe a part of her hindbrain warned her that every time she ate she felt sleepy, then flopped down, then didn't wake up for ages.

"Eat your food," he said. "You won't grow big and strong if you don't." He cringed at his dad's words coming out of his mouth. "Actually, if you don't eat, you'll die, and if you don't drink the juice, you'll die."

Her head must be so muddled. She didn't even flinch. He'd Googled about the dosage—he didn't want her death on his hands, despite telling Danika he'd kill the kid if he had to—and wondered if he'd been giving her too much.

"Do you miss your mummy?" He hadn't said it to be cruel but to get some sort of reaction. Anything. Something. "Do you wish you were at home?"

She fiddled with the doll's frilly dress.

"What do you and Mummy do all day?" He didn't imagine it was an awful lot. "You should be going to school soon. Are you looking forward to it?"

She didn't answer.

He picked up the sandwich and put it in front of her mouth, his irritation spiking. "Eat it."

She parted her lips and bit into the bread. He pried the doll from her fingers and lifted her hand to place it on the sandwich so she understood she had to hold it. He waited until she'd finished the whole thing, made sure she drank the carton of orange squash, then gave her one of the big-kid nappies he'd bought and told her to change the one she had one. He didn't want her pissing everywhere in her sleep. She handed the wet one to him. He placed it on the tray and left the loft.

He sat at his laptop, watching, and waited for her to fall asleep.

An hour later in his suit, wig, teeth, and beard, he was walking to Danika's location. She had no idea he'd added a tracker to her phone, back when he'd pretended to be a punter. She'd replied to a message then gone for a shower, leaving him to get dressed, and he'd grabbed the opportunity before her screen had locked.

She was at the Lantern. Good girl.

He thought some more about stiffing Purple. And smiled.

Chapter Six

Danika had done a three-hour shift at the Lantern and walked down the street, dreading going home. The evening had drawn in, a nippy bite to the air, and she drew her coat fronts across so they overlapped. She imagined Kenzie had taken her pill and was asleep by now. She also imagined the police combing through

CCTV on the roads surrounding Kenzie's house. She dreaded them discovering who The Organiser was; she didn't for one minute think he'd keep her name out of it if he got caught. She could pretend she didn't know what he was talking about and that she'd never met him in her life, but could she keep up the lies during an interview? She'd lied so much as it was that she *thought* she could handle it, but what if the pressure became too much and she broke down?

She crossed the street, going past parked cars belonging to punters. At the end, she turned the corner and saw him standing beneath a streetlight in his god-awful mac. What did he want *now*? Had he come to see whether she'd put the notes in the customers' pockets? She contemplated returning to the Lantern, taking advantage of the free work taxi to drop her home, but he'd just as likely turn up at her house later on. She may as well face whatever he had to say now, getting it over and done with.

She walked past him, and he pushed off the lamppost to stride alongside her. They didn't speak for a while, and she reckoned it was so the tension spiked, or maybe he was trying to scare her. She'd been frightened of him previously, but since she'd spoken to the twins, she had more confidence that someone had her back. Whether they'd have it if she revealed her situation was another matter, but surely getting Amelia home was more important than The Brothers having a go at her, maybe even giving her a Cheshire and banishing her from London. It had gone too far now, and earlier this evening, she'd made up her mind not to put the rumours in the pockets and to contact George and Greg, revealing everything. She'd suffer the consequences, something she should have done from the start.

Frustrated because The Organiser hadn't spoken, she said, "What do you want?"

"To see whether you've done what we discussed. I've told Purple that the rumours have been put in place. I doubt they'd like to find out that they haven't."

"That was a bit premature of you. I already told you about Cameron."

"You also told me you could put things in pockets even though he was there."

Shit, she'd forgotten she'd said that. "I did, but he shooed me off so I couldn't get to the coats. *He* was handing them out this evening."

"So have the twins decided to keep a guard at the house?"

"Yes. Widow said three men will take it in shifts. They want the women kept safe. They already provide taxis home so no one comes to any harm."

"So why haven't you got one? Why have they let you just walk out? What's so special about you that you can fend off any attackers? Or have they got someone watching you?" He turned back to look behind him, appearing nervous.

She liked seeing him off balance and on edge. "I told Widow I didn't want a lift, that I needed the walk. The fresh air. Although I would have taken a cab had I known *you'd* be out here."

"You sound pissed off that I chose to meet you after your shift."

"I'm pissed off that you always seem to know where I am and what I'm doing."

"I told you, I have eyes everywhere."

"I wish you were fucking blind," she muttered and walked faster.

"What did you just say?" He upped his pace to match hers.

"It doesn't matter. Anyway, I'm going to work ten minutes early tomorrow so maybe I can grab a chance to put the notes in the pockets then. I'll have to send the guard off for a cuppa or something."

"You'd better, because if Purple doesn't see the results anytime soon, they're going to be on my back again."

"When you think about it, that's not really my fault, is it? You were employed to do the job, not me. You were the one who chose me—so if I'm incompetent, that's your problem, not Purple's." She was being too brave, too uppity, especially as it was dark and no one was around to save her if he flipped his lid. "Sorry for snapping, but I'm tired. Can you please leave me alone now?"

He gripped her arm and stopped her from walking. "The way you're acting, you wouldn't believe your niece was being held somewhere."

"How do I even know she's still alive? You won't send me a picture. For all I know you could be lying and she's dead. You could have killed her the night you put her in your van."

"She isn't dead. She was fast asleep when I left her to come and meet you."

"What time was that? How long had you been waiting for me?"

He glared at her.

Danika thanked herself for putting on her flat-soled boots this evening. She'd made up her mind: she was going to follow him, see where he went, where he lived, or wherever Amelia was being kept. If she had an address she could go on, she could tell the twins who'd probably send their man, Will, to watch the property. She'd do that then send a message. She'd had enough. This had become bigger than she could handle.

"I'll see you soon," he said and strode down the street.

She walked after him slowly, keeping her distance until he vanished around a corner. She sped up and caught sight of him going down a residential street. She squinted. Did he have big over-ear headphones on? A rectangular light in his hand let her know he was holding his phone, so maybe he was listening to music. She kept close to the front gardens so if he looked as if he was going to turn around, she could quickly dart into one of them.

He kept going. They reached a road three streets away; detached houses, likely four bedrooms each, probably with conservatories, or what was it people had taken to calling them these days? Sunrooms. He disappeared down the side of number two into a dark slice of night, so she waited behind a tree at the entrance of the cul-de-sac in case he was hiding down there, waiting to pounce out at her. She didn't think he'd seen or heard her following him, but you couldn't be too sure, could you?

A downstairs light came on, so she assumed he'd gone inside. A silhouette appeared in the room beside the front door, and she recognised it as his. He closed the curtains, and she felt safe enough to dash along the pavement and dip down the side of the house. At the end was a tall wooden gate, and she searched for a knothole to look into the garden so she could get her bearings. Thankfully, a light was also on at the back, downstairs, illuminating a patio with a rattan sofa and chair set and a matching coffee table. To the left, fake grass bordered by rockeries behind low, white-stone walls. She wouldn't have had him down as a gardener, but if he was earning fifty grand for every job he did, maybe having a few jobs on the go at once, he could probably afford to pay someone to do it for him.

She slid her gaze to the gate handle, feeling for the iron ring. She twisted it, holding her breath in case it made a noise, then pushed the gate open a couple of inches, then a few more until she could poke her head around the edge.

Seeing no one, she crept into the garden and shut the gate. A blind had been half pulled down on the kitchen window. She bent to peer into the room. It had space for a dining area, although it was empty apart from a treadmill. He probably ate at the island which had two tan leather stools pushed beneath it. She ducked so she was lower than the windowsill and bent-walked towards French doors. She pressed the handle down, surprised the door opened. With her heart pounding, she felt inside her bag for her penknife and flipped the blade out. He could turn nasty if he caught her snooping, but it would certainly freak him out that she'd had the guts to follow him. He'd taken much pleasure in letting her know she'd never discover who he truly was, and she'd just proved him wrong.

She stepped inside and closed the door, for a moment contemplating going home. But what if Amelia was here? So she continued on, skirting the island and heading towards the door that led to the hallway. If she'd guessed right, he was in the room on the left. She strained her ear, picking up noises, at the same time spotting his suit jacket hanging on the newel post. Faint gunshots sounded, and shouts of pain followed. He must be watching a war film or something.

She sidled along until she reached the living room. She spied through the gap by the hinges. A man lay on a sofa in just his boxer shorts, his head bald, his eyes closed, his face clean-shaven. Was this his housemate? Or Amelia's babysitter? Had The Organiser gone upstairs to report back to Purple on his computer? She craned her neck to be able to see the television, and as she'd thought, a film played. Movement dragged her attention back to the man. He wiggled to get comfortable, folding his arms and tucking his hands beneath his opposing sides. She glanced at the floor in front of the sofa. His trousers and shirt in a pile on the carpet, plus a mound of hair.

What?

She suddenly remembered him mentioning whether his beard and hair were real. So *this* man was The Organiser? He looked scarier this way, more thuggish, and so much younger, like a kid dabbling in the dark web, presenting as some clever older man, when in fact, he was literally a lad of about twenty-three.

A snore popped out of him, but he was so devious, she worried he was faking it, that he knew she was there, because what kind of mastermind would leave their back door unlocked and then go to sleep? Or did he trust his neighbours not to break in?

She stood there for some time. It felt like half an hour but was probably only five minutes. He continued to snore softly, his mouth dropping open, his bottom lip rippling with his exhalations.

Fuck it, she was going to look upstairs.

She darted past the living room doorway and rounded the newel post, carefully checking his jacket pockets in case she found any identification—she wanted to know if his real name was Sebastian. They were empty. She placed her foot down on the first step and closed her eyes, praying it wouldn't creak. She did the same for each one until she'd counted twelve then opened her eyes and glanced down to make sure she was still alone.

He didn't stand at the bottom of the stairs.

She checked each of the rooms, and she'd been right, four bedrooms. One of them had an en suite. The place was neat and tidy—maybe he had a cleaner as well as a gardener. Beside the smallest bedroom was another set of stairs. They were wooden, the smell of fresh pine quite heavy, so were they new? Would *they* creak? Should she chance it? She had to really, didn't she? Amelia might be up there, hidden away in the loft, although would it be an average loft if there were proper stairs?

She climbed them, pausing halfway when one of them groaned. She waited, tense, for The Organiser to come bounding up and catch her, but nothing happened. She continued on to the top. This door was different to the others, it had a keyhole. If she hadn't seen a desk in one of the bedrooms, complete with a computer, she'd have thought he had an office up here, the lock so he could keep his nefarious business a secret. Maybe he did and the bedroom computer was for gaming. Now she'd seen what he really looked like, he seemed the type to play in his spare time.

Despite knowing in her heart the door would be locked, she turned the handle. She couldn't gain access, and even though she'd known she wouldn't, disappointment still crashed through her. She knelt on the little square landing and peered through the keyhole, one eye shut. A light was on, and all she could see was a cream wall.

She retreated down the stairs on her hands and knees so she could try to see beneath the door. Nothing but a wooden floor.

Something thudded, and she held herself still. Had it come from the loft room or downstairs? She cocked her head to listen properly, the pulse in her throat beating hard. A shuffling sound, like socks over laminate, then nothing. Danika's breath came out unsteadily, and she grappled to get control of it.

Someone coughed, but it wasn't a man.

Oh, Jesus Christ, that was Amelia.

Desperate to speak to her but too frightened to in case The Organiser woke and heard her, Danika, going against all of her instincts, backed down the stairs until she reached the other landing. She could try to find the key to the door. She could risk making too much noise and The Organiser catching her. She could leave this house and message the twins. Or go home and use the burner phone The Organiser had given her to phone the police, but she'd take it far away from her house in case they checked where the call had come from.

Going to the police risked him telling them what her involvement was.

The Brothers were her only chance of getting out of this without any accusations being levelled at her from Kenzie or the authorities, without charges being made against her—George and Greg would want to deal with her themselves, not hand her over to the coppers.

She composed herself, blinking away tears and stuffing down the guilt of leaving her niece behind. She tiptoed downstairs and, seeing he was still asleep, she made her way through the kitchen and back out into the alley beside the house. She took a moment to think about how she was going to put this to the twins. She was just going to have to come straight out with it, regardless of how it would make her look. If they punished her for this, then so be it, but at least Amelia would be home.

She emerged into the cul-de-sac, glancing to make sure the curtains were still closed in the living room, then jogged away around the corner, finding a safe enough space to use her phone. She stood in a red phone box that was now used for sharing books, took her mobile out, and typed in a message.

GODDESS: IT'S ME AGAIN. THERE WAS SOMETHING I NEVER TOLD YOU. I KNOW IT'S LATE, BUT CAN WE MEET? IT CAN'T WAIT UNTIL MORNING.

GG: FOR FUCK'S SAKE, WHAT NOW? CHRIST. WHERE ARE YOU?

She checked across the street for the road name.

GODDESS: FALCON CRESCENT. I'M IN THE PHONE BOX.

GG: WAIT THERE, WE WON'T BE LONG.

It was done. There was no turning back now.

Chapter Seven

Most of the time when The Organiser paid her a visit, he walked out of the shadows on the nights she was getting home from her escort agency work and frightened the life out of her by whispering right behind her. Other times he appeared in a supermarket or the little shop up the road, or even standing across the street. She reckoned it was so he could revel in being in charge, at the same time letting her know she could be being watched at any time.

She'd been at the escort agency for a while. On the previous time she'd seen him, he'd asked her how things were going and whether she'd had sex with any of the clients on the quiet. She hadn't, and if she had, she wouldn't be telling him anyway. Who knew whether he secretly worked for the Bainses. She couldn't trust anyone.

This evening, he stood across the road from her place, his hands in the pockets of his long coat, one of those macs with a belt. It was her night off from the agency, and she was on her way to the Orange Lantern for an interview, although he had no idea she'd set one up. He fiddled with his beard, something she'd noticed he did often, and leaned against a lamppost, the light from it giving him a creamy glow.

She crossed the road, and they walked along together as though friends, albeit not talking. He wouldn't do that until they'd got in his car. He'd parked it around the corner, and she sat in the back seat, never wanting to be in the front again. Last time she'd sat there, he'd felt it was okay to touch her leg up. Now he wasn't a paying customer, she didn't want him anywhere near her.

"Purple is getting understandably anxious," he said. "What are you even doing?"

"Once you gave me the phone number, I've been handing it out. What else am I supposed to do?"

"Remember I said you had to destroy the business by any means?"

"Yes.…"

"Then it's time to think outside the box, isn't it?"

She had to ask: "Do you know Mr and Mrs Bains?"

"Not personally, no. Why?"

"Because they took me to a warehouse."

"Did they now…"

"They've got another side to their business. It's sex parties, and they wanted me to work there. I said no. I'm going to have to stop working at the agency because I'm feeling too pressured to do something I don't want to do. On top of you telling me what to do."

"But if you stop working there, how are you going to do what Purple wants?"

"I don't know, but like you said, I need to think outside the box. I don't necessarily have to be there, do I."

"True. Where will you go?"

"I heard about an opening at the Orange Lantern. I've got an interview this evening. I can establish myself there while still working to ruin the agency."

She had no idea how she was going to do that, but she had to get away from Joseph and Farah. They were weird. And they scared her—Joseph had revealed that he hurt women, slashing crisscross marks over their faces with sharp knives. He'd shown his true personality after the first time she'd refused to work at their warehouse. The parties were massive orgies, where men could touch whoever they wanted and had sex in front of everybody else. Stages with cages around them protected sex worker dancers, but even they weren't off-limits. If a customer wanted to have sex with them, then they were allowed inside. When Danika had sex with her clients, it was in private and she could pretend the man loved her. If she closed her eyes, she could make out he was her husband. At the warehouse, it would feel too much like being used and abused.

"You'll be Daddy's best girl…"

She shuddered and caught sight of The Organiser's eyes in the rearview mirror. "I'm going to be late for my interview."

"Then I'll drop you off there. We can talk on the way." He licked his lips and started the engine. *"You look particularly gorgeous this evening."*

She shuddered again and stared outside at a row of cars opposite, all belonging to people with normal lives, coming home from their normal jobs. People she'd never be.

He eased out of his parking spot and headed in the direction of the Orange Lantern. "It'll be easier to ruin that business. Even I think bringing the escort agency down is too much of a big job for one person, but I'm sure, for little Amelia's sake, that you'll manage it somehow. You could even burn the building down."

He laughed a tad manically, as if arson was an actual viable answer. Maybe to him it was. Maybe to her it would be, too, if the reality of Amelia being kidnapped slapped her in the face. At the moment it was just a threat, something she could hold off, but what if he really did it? What if she couldn't do what Purple wanted in time?

"Or even torch the warehouse," he went on. "It's by the river, so you could set fire to it and escape via the arch tunnel. You'd be on a housing estate in no time, just one of the masses. Purple will be pleased when I tell them it's all gone up in smoke. A large sex

party really is a big draw and will definitely send some customers Purple's way."

She wanted to tell him she didn't give a fuck about Purple's clients or how anything affected their business. She wanted to scream at him, wishing she had a length of rope so she could loop it around his neck from behind his seat and pull really hard. She wanted him dead.

Maybe she should approach Kenzie and suggest they move away. Danika imagined they'd have to do it in the middle of the night and leave the majority of their possessions behind because, as The Organiser had already suggested, they were being watched. That could be a lie, of course, to keep her in line, but she still couldn't take the risk. And then there would be the issue of Kenzie asking questions as to why they had to leave London. What excuse could Danika give that was plausible enough to make her sister pack up and go without hesitation bar telling her about the threat to Amelia?

Would it just be easier to stay and do what The Organiser wanted?

He drew up at the end of a street and switched the engine off. "I'll wait here for you."

"There's no need," she said through gritted teeth. "I'd rather not go into the interview worrying about

you being outside. Please can you just let me do this on my own?"

He stared across at the brothel house. "I suppose so."

She got out and took her time walking towards the Orange Lantern, wanting to see him drive away first, plus she needed to get her thoughts in order. Farah and Joseph had become too pushy, and she really needed to secure this new job before she left the agency. She'd found that not having sex with clients was more difficult than she'd thought so really wanted this interview to be a success.

She should have married that lad when she was eighteen, then none of this would be happening. He'd proposed to her and everything, and afterwards, he'd gone to her family home and asked her father for permission. She hadn't told him they were estranged, she hadn't wanted to go into details about her childhood, and just knowing that Dad had been aware of an aspect of her life had her pulling away. Her boyfriend hadn't understood the sudden change in her, and she hadn't explained. He was better off without her anyway, so she'd ditched him and gone back to having sex with strangers, giving up her dream of ever living a normal life.

She took a deep breath and knocked on the door of the Orange Lantern. A woman with long hair and even longer legs answered, her outfit a basque, black stockings, and high heels. Earlier, Goddess had spoken to someone on the phone here. Was it her?

"Can I help you?" the woman asked.

"Hi, I'm Goddess and I've come for an interview."

"Oh, right. I'm Precious, and the interview will be with me, although I can already tell you'll be a brilliant fit here."

Danika stepped inside, guilt giving her a good old poke because she was here for all the wrong reasons. She followed Precious to an office and sent up a quiet prayer that she'd get the job. If she didn't, she wasn't sure what she'd do.

Goddess left the Lantern with a weight removed from her shoulders. She glanced up and down the street for The Organiser's car in case he'd been a creep and just pretended to drive away earlier, but it wasn't there. A dark-grey SUV was, though, one she'd seen before. Had it followed The Organiser's car when he'd dropped her off here? Had they been sitting in the SUV outside her bloody house before that? She'd have to ask

Oaklynn whether she'd seen them loitering around. They'd become friends recently, and Danika had told her about Joseph and Farah, how they'd been putting pressure on her. It had been good to talk about at least some of her problems, although their conversation had been interrupted a few times by Oaklynn's baby boy crying.

The SUV belonged to Joseph and Farah.

Danika put her head down and walked in the direction of home. Unfortunately, the SUV crawled along the road beside her, and she sensed the couple staring out at her. The whirr of a window going down gave her a split second's notice that they were going to speak to her.

"Getting yourself a new job, are you?" Farah called. "I trust you'll tell the punters there about our warehouse. On the quiet, of course."

Danika stopped walking and stared over at the car. "I'm not going to tell anybody about your fucking warehouse."

Joseph shook his head. "Why don't you get in the back and we'll have a little chat?"

Danika could have ignored him, but the menace in his eyes meant she did as she was told, despite his previous mentions of slashing women's faces. She felt so out of her depth, what with these two, The

Organiser, and whoever the fuck Purple was. Once she was in the car, Farah came to join her in the back. Joseph moved off and parked down the street in a space between lampposts. Danika's stomach rolled over at the thought of what they were going to do to her in the darkness.

"I'm handing my notice in," she blurted. "I have no more clients booked so I'm free to go."

"Of course," Farah said, "but I need you to prove that we can trust you. We can't just let you go with all that valuable information about us inside your head. You know quite a bit about the workings of the agency and the warehouse."

"I'm telling you, I'm not interested in causing you any hassle. I don't want to work at the warehouse, I've told you that, and the pressure you keep putting on me means I have to leave the agency. It's unfair what you've done to me."

It's unfair what I'm going to do to you, but I have no choice.

"Do us a little favour and we'll never bother you again."

She stiffened. "What favour?"

"Send the Orange Lantern clients our way."

She had a horrible thought. Was Purple either Farah or Joseph? The mention of sending clients over was the same thing Purple wanted. But hadn't The Organiser told her that if she saw Purple, she'd know why he'd called them that? Neither of these two favoured that colour, nothing related to purple stood out, so maybe what Farah had just said was a coincidence.

"And how do I do that?" Danika asked.

"You tell them about the parties but not where they are, and you give them a phone number and a code. That code will gain them entry into the warehouse."

"But how will they know where to go if I don't tell them?"

"Because of the phone number. We'll take care of everything once the clients contact us. All you need to do is give them the number and the code. Once you've done that for a little while, we may actually trust you and believe you won't cause us any problems. Oh, and get the sex workers to give you their phone numbers. We can approach them about jobs at the warehouse."

"Won't it look weird if I randomly ask for their numbers?"

"I don't care what it looks like, just get the job done. Would you like a lift home?"

It was pointless refusing because they knew where she lived anyway as she'd had to fill it out on her employment form. She may be cutting her nose off to spite her face, but she refused the offer. She got out and continued walking, relieved when the SUV drove by and turned a corner. That relief was short-lived. The Organiser's car came round the same corner and slowed to a crawl. He stared out at her then shot off again.

She had the urge to go to the scutty house and see if she could rent space there for the rest of the night, but someone else had probably snagged it by now. She needed the comfort of her old job so would give it a try. If a room wasn't available, she'd go to a familiar corner and pick someone up there.

With her world unravelling around her at an alarming rate, she continued her walk in the dark, alone and afraid.

Chapter Eight

George hadn't expected to be seeing Goddess so soon. The last time had been at the Noodle, where they'd had a fry-up and he'd put his point across in no uncertain terms that if people did them wrong, they paid for it. Even though he'd believed her story about Farah and Joseph, he still had Widow's warning ringing in his ears. The woman's instinct had been that Goddess was iffy, up her own arse a bit, and while he'd put that down to her involvement with Farah and Joseph, he hadn't allowed himself to fully trust her. He had to agree with Widow: Goddess was guarded, and it felt as if she'd still been playing her cards close to her chest despite the Bainses being dead.

So what was this all about then? Was she going to confess she'd done something wrong? Had she used George and Greg to kill Farah and Joseph before she handed over yet another problem for them to deal with? He had to remind himself she might not have done anything wrong. She may just need their help with something else, and maybe she'd kept it to herself so it didn't muddy the water regarding Farah and Joseph. That was a big enough job by itself, so he could forgive her for holding something else back. However, if that something turned out to be big, then he wouldn't be fucking happy. The question was whether he'd show her that anger or not.

Greg drove their taxi through the streets. Before they'd left home, they'd slapped beards and wigs on. George was ginger, like his Ruffian persona, and Greg was the preferred blond ZZ

Top lookalike. Goddess would know it was them because of the taxi, but the last time they'd been in disguise, their beards had been neatly trimmed, not big bushy long ones. Still, it didn't matter what they looked like, did it, it wasn't as if he was trying to impress her.

"What do you reckon she's going to dump on our plate now?" Greg asked.

"Fuck knows, but I was just about to go to bed before she sent that message, so it had better be something good. I was looking forward to a decent night's sleep an' all."

"Maybe she's caught wind of something at the Lantern."

"Well, it must be pretty ominous, otherwise, why say it can't wait till the morning? I don't like the sound of this."

"Me neither. How bad can it be, though, seriously?"

"I suppose. If it was bloody awful, surely she'd have come clean sooner."

Greg turned into Falcon Crescent and coasted along until he found the phone box. She stood inside amongst the books, light from a nearby streetlamp casting her in half shadow. She squinted through the glass, and at the toot of the horn, she came out and dashed across the street to get in the back of the cab. George left the passenger seat and got in the back with her.

Greg drove away and glanced at George in the rearview mirror, letting him know he'd stay out of this unless he felt it necessary to jump in. In other words, if George put his foot in it.

Goddess clipped her seat belt on and stared out of the side window at the passing scenery. Her chest rose and fell quickly, and she didn't seem herself at all.

"Has there been some kickback regarding Farah and Joseph?" George asked her. "Only, as far as we're aware, they've got no family and kept to themselves, so I doubt very much anybody even knows they're missing yet apart from their employees."

"No, it's not them, although they're something to do with it. Everything's linked together, and it's all such a fucking mess." Her voice hitched, and she laid a hand beneath her throat.

He recognised the sign—she was trying to compose herself, when all she wanted to do was blart her eyes out. "Go on then, spit it out."

She took a deep breath. "I expect you'll say I need punishing for not telling you sooner, and that for hiding something this big I deserve my face cut. I'm prepared for that to happen, because things have gone so far that I can't see any way out by myself. I've been warned not to tell you—or the police—and up until now I thought I could handle it, but I can't."

Warned? So someone was pulling her strings, were they? He rapidly went through what he knew about her but couldn't come up with anyone who'd be threatening her, because that's what this sounded like. There was her sister, then Oaklynn, her neighbour, but surely she wasn't anyone to worry about.

"What's happened?" he asked, keeping it gentle. He didn't want her to know his anger levels were rising—or that his Mad persona fancied a little outing.

She told her story, starting from when a punter called Sebastian—it might not be his real name—had forced her into working at the escort agency. He could be contacted on the dark web as The Organiser, and someone had asked him to ruin all the sex businesses in the area so they could snag the customers for themselves. George wasn't a massive brain box, but even he saw the flaw in that. People who used the likes of a posh agency were not the type to walk up to some tart on the street and ask for a blow job, so if this Purple client wasn't after top-end punters, then what was the point?

"It was taking me too long to work out a way to bring the agency and warehouse down," she said. "The Organiser was putting pressure on me, saying Purple was putting pressure on him. With that going on, as well as Farah and Joseph bullying me, trying to get me to work for them, I'd had enough, and the only way I could think to solve it was by telling you about Farah and Joseph. You could say I used you, and I did, but I didn't mean to do it maliciously. I couldn't tell you everything because I had The Organiser breathing down my neck."

"We've heard that name before."

"He said they all call themselves that, there's a few of them known as Organisers."

"Right. So I suspect now you're supposed to bring down the Lantern, then move on to The Angel and Kitchen Street."

"Yes, but I can't do it. I love working at the Lantern. Even though Widow looks at me as if I'm weird, I like her and don't want to ruin her life. If the Lantern went down, she'd be gutted."

"So why not tell this Organiser bastard to fuck off and be done with it?"

Greg tutted. "It doesn't sound like it's as easy as that, bruv."

George conceded the point. This bloke had likely scared her into doing as she was told. "Where do things stand with him now?"

"He wants me to spread rumours to the customers that the Lantern women have sexual diseases. I was supposed to do it this evening but didn't. When I finished work, he was waiting for me and asked if I'd done it or not. I admitted I hadn't and blamed it on Cameron being there. But that's not the worst of it. Because I was taking so long, weeks, to ruin the agency and warehouse, he told me if I didn't get a move on he'd kidnap my niece."

Just going by her tone, George knew what she was going to say next. "He kept his promise, didn't he?"

She nodded, still looking out of the window. "It was so much to keep to myself. Too much going on at once. I couldn't cope. And then when he took Amelia, I knew he wasn't messing about. I mean, I knew before, but then I *really* knew."

"So what's happening there? Do the police know she's gone or is your sister in on it with you?"

"That's the part I feel guilty about the most: she's got no clue I'm involved. The police don't suspect me, they've said so, and I had an alibi anyway."

"So how come this hasn't been on the news?"

"The police are trying to keep it low-key so the kidnapper doesn't know what they're up to. It's had a few lines in online newspapers, but it's so weird, even the residents in her street haven't said anything on their newsfeeds. Maybe the police told them not to, I don't know. But anyway, I followed him tonight. I'd had enough and wanted to see if he was going to visit Amelia. He went into a house, so I crept round the back and went inside." She told them what she'd done and that she was convinced the girl was in the loft. "I just left her there. What the hell kind of auntie am I?"

"You actually did the right thing," George said. "If you'd let him know you were there, if you'd tried to take her, you might also be locked in that loft. It would be easy enough for him to find someone else to spread rumours about the Lantern. Where's the house?"

"Number two Piper Avenue."

George took his phone out and set up a group chat with Ichabod, Will, and Cameron.

GG: I WANT YOU AT PIPER AVE, NUMBER TWO. ONE RESIDENT, CURRENTLY BALD AND ONLY IN BOXERS, ASLEEP ON SOFA, BUT THAT STATUS MAY HAVE CHANGED. HE COULD NOW HAVE HAIR, BE BEARDED, SO BE ON YOUR GUARD. POSSIBLE FOUR-YEAR-OLD CHILD INSIDE THE LOFT, A GIRL, AMELIA. TAKE HER TO THE BIGGEST SAFE HOUSE. I WANT HIM PICKED UP, BUT NO TAKING HIM TO THE WAREHOUSE BECAUSE OF THE NEW CCTV THERE. ICHABOD, YOU'RE IN CHARGE OF HIM, AND YOU KNOW WHERE HE NEEDS TO BE. EVERYONE COVER YOUR FACES. WE CAN'T RISK THE CHILD BEING ABLE TO GIVE YOUR DESCRIPTIONS TO THE POLICE. EXPLAIN PROPERLY WHEN I HAVE MORE TIME.

"She'll be collected as soon as possible," he said to Goddess. "I've got men on their way there now. I'll let you know when the kid's been extracted."

At last, she turned to face him. The light from streetlamps lit the tears running down her cheeks. "Then what happens?"

"She'll be taken to the safe house, the one you stayed at. Then we've got to work out how we can get her back home without the police seeing us. I don't want to leave her in the street somewhere when she's already been through a traumatic experience. It's better that you're not the one to take her home either. The police do *not* need to know of your involvement. It just means keeping her away from her mother for a few more hours while we work something out."

"What will you do to me?"

"I'm not even thinking about you at the minute. We have a kid to return and a bloke to murder, plus whoever this Purple fucker is, so that's quite enough to busy my mind at the moment, thank you. You carry on as normal. Act surprised when Amelia goes home."

"Isn't there something I can be doing to help?"

"With the police possibly keeping an eye on you, it's probably better that you just go to work and live normally. Remember where you are and what you're doing at all times so when they ask you for an alibi when Amelia's found, it's airtight."

"There's something else."

He had the urge to thump the seat between them. "What?"

"I need help killing my father."

"Oh, fuck me sideways." He sighed and pinched the bridge of his nose. "One thing at a time, all right?" He thought about that for a minute—his curiosity was too high for him not to know. "Actually, what do you need him dead for?"

"Childhood sexual abuse. I'll tell you everything after Amelia's safe. Will you be able to find out who Purple is? The Organiser speaks to them on his computer."

"Yeah, we'll get that sorted." George took his phone out again.

GG: Need laptops, computers, and any other online devices removed from the property and taken to our digital bloke.

He let out a long breath, shaking his head at the influx of information swirling in his mind. "Right, as this was sprung on us, we're going to have to drop you off now and go somewhere to get our heads around this. We need to plan how we get Amelia home. Don't worry, we'll sort it. Just remember to stick by your usual routine."

She stared out of the window again, scrubbing at her cheeks. He honestly didn't know what to say to her regarding keeping such a big secret. She'd basically helped a criminal on their Estate, but he could hardly slash her face for it when she'd been forced into it. Maybe that's what Widow had sensed when she'd got hold of them to say Goddess was 'off', that there was something about her she couldn't put her finger on. George and Greg had put that down to Goddess being frightened of Farah and Joseph, but what if she was willingly working for The Organiser and coming to them now was part of their plot? What if The Organiser was waiting at the house, knowing full well she was going to ask for help and they'd send someone round there? Thank God all of their men wore bulletproof vests now. Since Greg had been shot, George had insisted on it. If The Organiser had a gun…

He'd give her one more chance to come clean.

"I need you to tell me if you're not on the level," he said, his voice loud on purpose so he got her full attention. "If this is some bullshit tactic between you and The Organiser, then it's better you say so now. Actually, Greg, pull over. We'll wait here until we get news of whether there's a little girl in that house or not. If there isn't, then Miss Goddess can come to the cottage with us."

Chapter Nine

The Organiser had woken from his nap and gone into the kitchen to make some sandwiches. He needed more than something between two slices of bread, and so did Amelia, but he didn't have any energy to cook, nor could he be bothered to ring for a Domino's. He chose Nutella for her—he'd bet she liked chocolate spread—and piled layers of ham, lettuce, and tomatoes in his. He laid a couple of chocolate chip cookies from the Tesco bakery on a plate, then added a bottle of water for him and a juice carton for her. They could have a little picnic.

His stomach rumbled.

He wasn't going to drug her tonight, she had enough in her system as it was to keep her groggy. He'd sleep in the loft with her later so if she woke up and made a noise he could shut her up quickly. He wasn't a paedo, so he'd put a wall of pillows down the middle of the king-sized bed. It would be more comfortable for her than the way she kept falling asleep on the rug.

If he was a nicer person, he'd have lifted her onto the bed instead of leaving her on the floor, but he wasn't nice, was he? Or he tried not to be.

"Niceness doesn't get you anywhere, son."

He carried the tray upstairs and paused on the landing. He sniffed the air and then himself, swearing he could smell Danika's perfume. Maybe the scent was still up his nose from when he'd been with her earlier. He continued on the second set of steps and took the key off the tray, inserting it, twisting it.

A tap and a thud had him pausing to listen, all his senses on high alert. Amelia must have woken up. She was probably pretending to walk her Barbie across the floor. He turned the handle and opened the door enough that he could poke his head round to check where she was. She was still on the rug, but the en suite door was open, so she must have taken the nappy off and been to the toilet.

She idly looked up at him and then back down at her doll. He was beginning to wonder whether it was the drugs doing this to her or if she was generally apathetic in nature. Did she have a quiet personality and was a bit introverted? Had Kenzie left the kid to her own devices for the most part? Wasn't Amelia mentally stimulated enough to give a shit? She hadn't even changed the Barbie's dress, yet he given her several outfits to choose from, plus a few pairs of shoes and some tiny plastic handbags.

What was up with her?

He locked the door and approached her, once again sitting cross-legged on the rug.

"Here." He pointed to the plate with half a sandwich on it plus a cookie.

At last, she had some kind of reaction other than blankly staring. She reached out for the biscuit and took a bite.

"Mummy makes these when she's not poorly."

Her speaking took him by surprise. He picked up his sandwich and bit into it. Chewed and swallowed while he thought about how to answer her. "I wish my mummy had made them, but she left me as soon as I was born."

That was probably too much information, but he'd said it now, couldn't take it back. He never spoke about Mum. Dad didn't want to discuss her, and The Organiser found it too difficult to accept she'd abandoned him. Why he'd just told this kid about her was anyone's guess.

"What's wrong with your mummy?" he asked.

"She cries a lot and sleeps a lot. She forgets to make dinner sometimes, but it's okay because Auntie Danika comes and buys pizza and chicken fried rice."

"Do you like Auntie Danika?"

"She's all right."

It seemed she'd had enough talk for now as she steadily munched on her biscuit until it was all gone. She struggled to take the drink straw out of the plastic wrapper. He found it difficult to watch her fumbling fingers. He looked away, glad to finally hear the pop of the straw going inside the carton. He faced her again, watching her drink, wondering what was going through her little head. He scratched his, realising that for the second time with her, he'd forgotten to put his wig and beard on. He couldn't imagine their paths would ever cross once she'd gone home, but who knew if the one time he went into town, she was there and spotted him, calling out that he was the man who'd hidden her in his house.

He was going to have to be cruel to her to save his own skin.

"You'll go back to your mummy soon, but you must never tell her, the police, or Auntie Danika where you've been and who you were with. If you do, I'll know and I'll come back and kill you."

She lowered one of her fingers to cover a biscuit crumb on her knee. She sat like that for some time, then stared him straight in the eyes. "It's okay, I won't say nuffin' if you give me a cuddle when I can't sleep. I like it here, and you're nice to me."

An unexpected lump swelled in his throat. Stupid fucking kid. He thought she'd have hated it here, that she'd know she'd been locked away, but perhaps she was so used to staying at home with her mother all the time that this really wasn't any different, except for the fact he remembered to feed her. A part of him was worried about returning her to a mum who may not be the best.

"The minute you take on other people's problems, they become your own, son."

He nodded. It was for the best he didn't get involved. He'd leave the kid outside her house at some point, so long as Danika finished all of her jobs. The thing was, she needed to get a move on, because he didn't like the responsibility of having the child in his house. He'd kidnapped her far too early, should have waited until the Orange Lantern had closed down at least, but he'd been too desperate to prove a point to get Danika to heel.

"Eat your sandwich," he said.

"Because I won't get big and strong if I don't." She grinned up at him, her nose scrunching.

Fucking hell, the last thing he needed was to get attached to her. Who'd have thought that would happen? He glanced away from her again until she'd finished her food and drink, then he collected the tray and walked over to the door. He'd changed his mind about sharing the bed with her now, about not drugging her. It was best to distance himself, only dealing with her at meal times.

He opened the door and stepped out onto the little landing, locking up and going down the stairs. As he headed along the hallway towards the kitchen, another tap and thud had him pausing his steps. He'd kept the light on in the kitchen when he'd left it, but now it was dark. Maybe the bulbs had blown in the fancy chandelier hanging over the island.

What, all of them?

He sniffed again. It wasn't Danika's perfume this time but somebody's aftershave. He turned slowly to look at the front door, but the chain was across, so no one had come in that way. He faced the kitchen doorway again, straining an ear: was that his breathing or someone else's? He stepped forward a few paces, then stopped on the threshold, staring outside beneath the bottom of the blind on the window. As the living room light spilled out of the room behind him, he couldn't see outside properly, mainly the reflection of his lower half. At least no one was behind him, but he wished he'd popped his head into the living room on his way past to check if anyone was there.

Because someone was.

He gripped the tray tight enough on either end that he could use it as a shield should anyone jump out at him. He moved into the kitchen slowly, assessing the darkness, the shadows, the corners, the everything. As far as he could make out, no one was there, but what about under the island? Had those stools been pulled out a bit to accommodate a person? Was that what those taps and thuds had been? He couldn't be sure from this angle.

He lowered the tray to the worktop, clenching his fists to use those as weapons instead, then walked around the island, darting into a bent-over position to check beneath.

No one there.

The smell of aftershave was stronger here, something lemony overlaid with spice. He hadn't used any products since the cleaner had been, and that was three days ago, so he couldn't blame it on any sprays. Nervous, and if he were honest, a little scared, he backed towards the way he'd come, keeping an eye on his reflection in the lower half of the kitchen window.

Still no one standing in the hallway.

Unless they were hiding in his little toilet beside the front door, the living room, or upstairs…

He reached up and flipped the light switch. The chandelier sprang to life, so either somebody had switched it off after he'd gone upstairs with the tray or he was going mental and hadn't realised he'd done it himself.

But that didn't explain the smell.

He turned to face the front door, bracing himself to go in the living room then search the rest of the house. He stretched his hand out to his right to open the drawer beneath the microwave, cautiously feeling around in there until his fingers curled around the handle of a knife. If it turned into a bloodbath in here, he'd have to deal with the mess afterwards. Whoever had dared to come in his house would get the shock of their lives when they bumped into him.

He slowly walked down the hallway on high alert, his heart thumping, his chest tight. What if Danika had followed him here? He'd definitely smelled her perfume, so it wasn't that far-fetched an idea. What if she'd phoned someone for help and it was their aftershave he could smell? But where were they? Had they left or were they still here?

He stepped into the living room, glancing around, quickly coming to the realisation he was alone. He yanked the curtains across on the bay window in case someone stood in the space behind them, but it was empty. He peered outside, leaning his forehead on the glass, keeping his free hand curved at the side of his head to block out his reflection so he could see clearly. He looked for unfamiliar cars, but his gaze landed on a familiar one.

The red one Danika had been dropped home in.

He took a step back, his lungs seizing. He closed the curtains. Poked himself in the forehead several times with his eyes closed, trying to work out what the *fuck* to do now. She must have contacted The Brothers. She'd said the man in the red car had looked after her at the safe house. She'd actually had the balls to ask them for help.

He hadn't realised she was so overwhelmed. Yes, she'd told him as much, but he thought he'd scared her enough that she'd do whatever he said, no matter what.

Was she sitting in the back of the red car, only he couldn't see her? Had she been in this house and discovered Amelia was here, and they were now waiting for the twins to come in and collect her?

He went through his options. He could quickly get dressed and walk away via the back alley before they even knew he'd left—unless they were in his back garden. He could take the little girl home in his van, throw her out on the pavement, and go into hiding for a while. Because that was all the twins would want, wasn't it, for Amelia to be returned to her mother? Yes, they'd want to punish him for kidnapping her, but if he hid for long enough, they might forget all about him.

Don't be so stupid.

He checked the toilet and, finding it empty, went upstairs. In his bedroom, he put the knife on the bed and grabbed his tracksuit, putting it on and stuffing his feet into socks and trainers. He walked into his office, switching the light on and staring in shock at his desk.

No computer or laptop.

Fuck.

Someone had been here while he'd either slept or was in the loft with Amelia. Or both. The man in the red car was probably keeping watch so someone else may still be in the house.

He wasn't sure his legs were going to keep working. They'd gone to jelly, and he felt so cold. Fear gripped him hard, and he stumbled into the bathroom. Empty. The other two bedrooms. Empty. He poked his head round the wall to look up the stairs towards the loft.

The door was open.

The sound of an engine had him rushing to the front bedroom window and pulling the curtain open a tiny bit so he could look out but they couldn't fully see him. The red car was driving away, and someone was in the back. A man. Was Amelia with him?

He had to get the hell out of here. He spun to launch himself towards his chest of drawers, yanking open the top one and grabbing hold of his passport. He stuffed it in a backpack and added another change of clothes, plus an emergency envelope full of cash. He turned to head towards the door and freedom, but the Irish bloke who ran Jackpot Palace filled the frame — the very man he'd had to pay the fifty grand to that he'd got from Purple, to repay the gambling debt.

"Where the feck do ye think *ye're* goin'?"

Chapter Ten

Ichabod glanced at the knife on the bed then back at the eejit calling himself The Organiser. He wasn't sure he was in the mood to get him to see sense, but he supposed he'd better give him a warning. "I wouldn't bother if I were ye."

The bloke stared at him, giving off spoilt brat vibes. "But you're not me, are you?"

What a smug twat. I might ask tae hang around and watch him get offed. "And I'm feckin' glad about that. I wouldn't want tae be known as someone who went round abductin' little girls. What are ye, a feckin' paedo?"

He shook his head, appearing horrified, the accusation hitting him hard, as was the intention. "Fuck off, no! It's not what you think."

"It doesn't matter what I think, I'm just here tae collect ye."

"For the twins? Did they find out it was me who owed the money?"

"I don't have tae answer that—statin' the obvious gets on my tits. If ye don't want tae get hurt, I suggest ye walk very slowly towards me and don't even think about pickin' up that knife. Even if ye do, I'll have it out of your hand within seconds. And let's have a proper name, shall we? I don't want tae have tae keep callin' ye The Organiser—it's like somethin' I'd have on my desk in the office. So who are ye? I don't recall ever gettin' ye name out of ye when ye legged it from the casino owin' all that money, nor when ye dropped it at the back door wid a note inside the bag sayin' it was from ye. I'll let ye know now, the twins are goin' tae be pissed off it's ye. That's an extra bone they'll have tae pick."

"Fuck, I paid it back, so surely…"

"Name."

"You can call me Sebastian."

"I doubt that's real."

"You doubt right."

"Okay then, Not Really Sebastian, like I said, come slowly towards me."

"Tell me where they've taken the kid first."

"Ye're not really in a position tae bargain wid me, but I'll indulge ye. She'll be kept safe until she can be returned tae her mammy."

"And what about Danika? What's going to happen to her? She knew all about the kidnap, you know. Don't let her fool you into thinking she was nothing to do with this."

"What she has and hasn't done is feck all tae do wid me. I've been given instructions tae pick ye up and take ye tae a cottage. Whatever else is goin' on isn't somethin' we need tae concern ourselves with. Now either ye leave this house wid me quietly or ye leave it loudly when my flick-knife goes in ye back."

Sebastian seemed to come to a decision. "You need to let Purple know you've taken me."

"What the fuck are ye talkin' about?"

"I need to speak to the twins. They have to understand that Purple must know where I've gone."

"Ye can explain it all tae George and Greg. They'll be meetin' us at their cottage. If ye want my advice, if ye were forced into whatever is ye've been doin', ye're better off admittin' that and droppin' the other person in the shite. Ye might just end up wid broken legs and a missin' arm for ye trouble, they might not actually kill ye."

"Fuck."

"Ye're in big pretty bad trouble, so ye need tae start thinkin' of ways tae lessen ye punishment. I mean, I can start it here and now if ye want me tae, I'm a black belt in several martial arts, but I'd advise against it. Ye need all ye strength at the cottage."

Sebastian dropped his backpack as if resigned to his fate. "I'm not going unless you promise to tell Purple I've been taken."

"I promise tae tell Purple ye've been taken, or I promise tae ask the twins tae tell Purple ye've been taken. Now can we feckin' go because ye're doin' my bastard head in."

Ichabod was surprised the man stepped forward, but he wasn't surprised that his gaze flicked towards the knife on the bed. Ichabod took his out of his waistband and released the blade. He raised his eyebrows.

"Ye can try me if ye want."

Sebastian closed his eyes, took a deep breath, and came forward the rest of the way. Oddly, he turned his back on Ichabod and placed his wrists together at the bottom of his spine. This was rare for anyone to voluntarily ask to be cuffed; Ichabod had anticipated a struggle in that respect. He put his blade away and slipped the knife in his pocket, taking out a cable tie and securing the man's wrists. He spun him round to face the door.

"Go downstairs."

Sebastian left the room and glanced towards the other stairs at the end of the landing. He then went down the others, muttering, "I'm sorry, Dad."

Ichabod followed him. "Will he be disappointed in ye?"

"Yeah."

"Would it be better for him if ye just went 'missing'?"

"No, he'd rather know the truth. He needs to know it."

Sebastian waited by the front door. All the fight seemed to have gone out of him. Maybe he'd realised that when it came to being apprehended by one of The Brothers' men, you were well and truly fucked.

He left the house without complaint, quietly, and got in the back of Ichabod's stolen car, one of several that were kept behind the back of Jackpot Palace in the private car park, stolen by the twins' thief, Dwayne. Ichabod took another cable tie out of his pocket and looped it through the other one, securing Sebastian to the interior handle above the door, the one Ichabod usually used to hang up his suits and shirts. He got in the front seat and drove away, not worrying about Sebastian seeing where he was going because he doubted the man would be coming out of the cottage alive.

"What's the cottage?" Sebastian asked.

"Exactly what it sounds like, a cottage."

"And what happens there?"

"Ye'll basically get tortured until ye spill the beans."

"Purple needs to be there, too. They can't get away with this. It's their fault I'm in this position."

"That old chestnut. Why do people always blame someone else? Why can't they accept responsibility for their own actions?"

"I swear to you, it's all Purple's fault."

"Well, I'm sure the twins will enjoy listenin' tae your story. I wish ye luck there, that's all I can say."

They continued the journey in silence. Ichabod turned onto the track that led to the woods and parked outside the cottage, the twins' taxi there. He imagined they'd already prepared the steel room, and he didn't envy them the headache of trying to work out how to get the little girl back home without anyone seeing. He'd offer to do it himself but knew how arsey George could get if anyone poked their nose in. He'd wait to be asked if, indeed, they chose him.

"Come on. Let's get inside." He undid his seat belt, and on his way round to let Sebastian out, he flicked the blade from his knife and used it to cut the cable tie off the handle.

Sebastian remained where he was for a moment, staring ahead at the cottage, then he glanced across at the woods as if taking in his final sights. It had to be difficult to know you were going to be killed. Or was he contemplating making a run for it?

"I suggest ye get a move on. If they have tae come out tae get ye, it'll make them angrier than they already are."

Ichabod steered him to the cottage and knocked on the door. It opened, revealing Greg in the frame. Maybe George didn't trust himself with this lad just yet.

"He wants ye tae know that Purple needs talkin' tae."

"Right."

"Do ye need anythin' else from me?"

"Possibly. We'll be in touch. Ditch the car, and if we need you later, use another one from you know where."

Ichabod nodded and returned to the car. He reversed down the track then stopped to send a text message, one he hadn't sent earlier because he couldn't afford to be distracted in front of Sebastian.

ICHABOD: HE'S THE FELLA WHO OWED US FIFTY GRAND AND PAID IT BACK. JUST THOUGHT YOU SHOULD KNOW.

With no response, he continued his journey back to Jackpot Palace.

Chapter Eleven

Tonight, Danika had decided to go round and visit Kenzie and Amelia. She had the evening off from the Orange Lantern. A few nights ago, she'd gone there so Precious could show her how things worked prior to starting her first shift the next day. They'd talked for some time, Danika lying, saying she'd been brought up in Bermondsey by nice parents who'd died in a car crash. She'd added to the lies by saying she'd gone off the rails, turning to coke to get her through the grief, then sorting herself out by joining the escort agency. She'd claimed the work there was too bland and had admitted that she needed sex so she could pretend men loved her. Precious hadn't commented on any of it, as though she had zero empathy, which had been disconcerting.

Danika wondered if deep down she wanted to tell Kenzie what was going on but beg her not to phone the police or The Brothers. Maybe if she explained the enormity of the situation, Kenzie would be happy to move away. But something told Danika to keep it to herself. It was too dangerous with The Organiser plus Farah and Joseph in her life. She felt hemmed in on all sides, and with the pressure of having to be Goddess at the Lantern, handing out phone numbers and codes to the clients, hoping to God they didn't grass her up to Widow or Precious for it, she had too many spinning plates in the air. One of them was going to drop and smash soon, she knew it.

Maybe being with Kenzie would give her the illusion that life wasn't so fraught with danger, even if only for a couple of hours, but she was kidding herself. Going to Kenzie's meant facing a whole new problem.

She knocked on the front door armed with a carrier bag full of snacks and drinks. Kenzie opened the door and stared at her, looking rough as arseholes, as if she hadn't had a shower or a change of clothes in days. She wandered off to the living room without saying a word.

Oh God, she was clearly in one of her depressive states. Danika entered the house and slipped the chain on, double locking the door, reminding herself to tell Kenzie to always lock up properly when she was home. She stood in the hallway and glanced at the state of the living room. Kenzie hadn't tidied up, not for some time. A wonky pile of clothes, that had perhaps once being folded, lurched on the armchair. The floor, covered in Amelia's toys, barely had any carpet on show. The bits that were visible appeared not to have been hoovered for ages, crumbs and God knew what else nestling between the fibres.

Kenzie lay on the sofa under a pink fleece blanket, although calling it pink was a stretch; beige was a better description because it needed a bloody good wash. Amelia sat on the floor, her head down, staring at her dolly. Sometimes Danika wondered whether Kenzie let the place get in a state because she knew her sister would tidy it.

Sighing, Danika took the carrier bag into the kitchen. It was pointless unpacking it yet because this room was a mess, too.

"Have you two had any dinner?" she called.

"I haven't been feeling well," Kenzie shouted.

Danika rolled her eyes. "I'll get us a takeaway in then, shall I?"

With no response, she got on with ordering a pizza to be delivered, then she changed it so there was enough food for tomorrow as well. Thankfully Kenzie had a slimline dishwasher, so Danika unloaded it and put things away, then filled it again and set it on a quick-wash cycle. She tidied, wiped the worktops, popped all the stuff heaped on the dining table into an empty washing basket for now, so they at least had somewhere to sit and eat. She made them a cuppa each and carried them into the living room. Kenzie took hers and sat up to drink it, watching Danika clean her living room as though it were a normal occurrence.

Which it was.

"What's been up with you, then?" Danika asked, refolding the tower of washing and putting it in piles on the coffee table, which was surprisingly clear of debris.

"It's these fucking migraines," Kenzie said. "It's the stress of not having enough money to manage.

Amelia will need new clothes and shoes to start school soon. Where the hell's that supposed to come from?"

This was also a normal occurrence, the same conversation they had every time Danika visited, which was why, before she got here, she always put money in an envelope to leave beside the kettle for her sister to find. She felt so guilty that Kenzie's life was such a mess compared to hers, but then again, look at the mess Danika's life was in now. It was no longer a question of just dealing with what she did with her body. The shameful guilt of that, the trying to understand why she continued to do it. Now she had The Organiser, Joseph and Farrah, and then there was Widow who kept looking at her funny. Had she sensed Danika was up to something? Did she work for Purple, too, or even The Organiser?

Danika was aware paranoia was taking over, but his situation was so bloody scary. It wasn't any surprise that she might be seeing things that weren't there. She hadn't imagined Widow staring at her, though. She'd caught her doing it a few times.

"I'll sort the money, you know that," Danika said. "Have you been to the doctor about the headaches?"

"Yeah, and he's doing fuck all about it. I personally think it's hormone related. I've been Googling."

I'm surprised she hasn't convinced herself she's got a brain tumour. "Have you tried Paramol tablets? They're really good."

Kenzie sighed. "I've tried everything."

Of course you have. *Danika wasn't sure why she bothered trying to help her. Every suggestion was met with a roadblock or reason why she couldn't do this or that. It was tiring to deal with her in these kinds of moods, especially when she had so much else on her mind. Then she felt bad for thinking that. It wasn't Kenzie's fault Danika had issues. Then again, it wasn't Danika's fault Kenzie had them either.*

Danika kept her thoughts to herself and continued tidying up. The whole time Amelia had been playing, she hadn't once glanced up at her auntie. Not for the first time, Danika wondered whether all was okay with the little girl. She seemed insular, didn't smile or laugh like other children. She reminded Danika of herself and Kenzie as kids, although she doubted very much that Amelia would be doing anything for a daddy figure like they'd had to do — that was one thing Kenzie would never allow. Maybe her niece's behaviour was a direct result of Kenzie's. Danika had often pondered whether she should anonymously contact social services, but the guilt of that would he eat her alive.

With the room as tidy as she could get it, considering there weren't any storage places to put a lot of the things, Danika drank her lukewarm coffee then took both their cups into the kitchen. The doorbell rang, and she turned to walk down the hallway to answer it, but Kenzie got there first.

"Why the fuck's the chain on?" Kenzie snarled and wrenched it across so she could open the door.

Because I need to keep you both safe.

Danika held her breath as she stared at the person on the doorstep. Thank God they had a cap on with the logo of the pizza company on the front. She stepped forward to peer over Kenzie's shoulder into the street, checking in case someone sat in a car watching the house. She couldn't see anyone so let Kenzie take the pizza boxes and wander to the kitchen. Danika thanked the delivery driver, shoved a fiver in his hand, shut the door, and put the chain on again. She stood in the living room doorway and looked down at Amelia.

"Come on, there's pizza for dinner."

Amelia got up and, with her head down, walked beside Danika down the hallway.

"What's up, munchkin?" Danika ruffled her hair.

"Nuffin'."

Danika wasn't about to push her on it, and besides, they were in the kitchen now, and Kenzie would have a go at her for probing. Her sister had already opened two of the boxes and was stuffing pizza in her face. Danika stared at her, upset by how selfish she was, sorting out her own hunger before her daughter's.

Danika helped Amelia settle at the table with two slices of pizza, then she went to her carrier bag and took out cans of pop and a small carton of orange squash. She stabbed the straw in the top of the carton and handed it to Amelia. Then she sat and selected a piece of pizza herself, hoping that her actions would penetrate Kenzie's mind and tell her that was the way you were supposed to behave when there was a child in your care.

What had happened to Kenzie lately for her to be like this? She'd always had depressive sessions but not as frequently as they'd been happening lately.

"Did you get anti-depressants sorted?" Danika asked.

Kenzie nodded.

"Do you think they're the right type for you?"

Kenzie frowned. "What the fuck kind of question's that?"

"What I'm trying to say is you're not yourself and haven't been the last few times I've been round. So do you think it's the tablets making you not want to do the housework and sort Amelia out and whatever?"

Kenzie blinked across at her daughter as if seeing her in a different light. The poor kid had grubby clothes on, had maybe worn them for days. Her hair was matted and all over the place, her face not only covered in pizza sauce now but what might be dried chocolate spread.

"I'm going to be blunt, Kenzie. She shouldn't look like that, should she."

Tears rolled down Kenzie's face. "I try so hard, but nothing ever seems to get done. If I tidy up, she messes it straight away."

"Maybe get her to help you tidy up? Or have a rule where there's one toy out at a time. If she wants another, she has to put the first one back."

Kenzie snorted. "Since when did you become Mother of the Year?"

"I didn't. It's just common sense."

They continued eating without further conversation, and afterwards, with the leftover pizza put in the fridge for tomorrow, Danika offered to bathe Amelia, knowing full well she'd probably have to scrub the bath first.

She left Kenzie to her moping and took the little girl upstairs. The bathroom was also a state, and while Amelia sat on the floor and played with some rubber ducks, Danika got on with cleaning. Once that was done, she filled the bath with a few inches of water. Amelia splashed around in there for a good half an hour while the hair conditioner did its work. Danika managed to untangle the damp bird's nest using a wide-tooth comb.

As she was drying Amelia, she asked, "Are you looking forward to starting school?"

Amelia nodded.

Sensing it was pointless trying to get the girl talking, she found her some clean pyjamas, miraculously, and straightened out the untidy bedroom. She glanced into Kenzie's and, much as she wanted you just leave her sister to wallow in her own junk, she thought maybe having it tidied would help her mental health.

She's doing it on purpose, don't forget. She knows you'll tidy when you get here.

Kenzie had always been the more selfish of the two. She'd probably only had Amelia so she had someone to love, although she wasn't showing much sign of doing that at the moment. Danika was going to have to get brutal and give her a few home truths.

She went downstairs and pulled the hoover out of a jumble of other paraphernalia in the cupboard under the stairs. The dust catcher was full, so she emptied that, discovering the kitchen bin was bursting so she emptied that, too. She gave downstairs a hoover then made a coffee, taking it into the living room to her sister.

Amelia had fallen asleep on the armchair, so Danika was safe to say what she had to say. She wanted to scream at having to cope with Kenzie's shitty attitude when she'd come here to clear her mind for a few hours, not this fucking house.

"If anyone came in here and saw the state of this place and your child, social services would likely become involved."

Kenzie shrugged. "No one ever comes here apart from you, so it doesn't matter."

"I'm just trying to make a point that if someone sees the state of your life, they might start asking questions as to whether you can look after Amelia properly. I can see that you're not. Have you been taking her out when she's got a dirty face and messy hair?"

"I get our shopping delivered and don't go out at the moment if I can help it. The migraines…"

There didn't seem to be any evidence of a migraine this evening, but Danika supposed Kenzie could be hiding the pain. Maybe she was being too quick to judge. She had no idea what it was like to care for a child, the demands put on you as a mother. She had no right to look down her nose at Kenzie.

"How will you get her to school if you're not going out?"

Kenzie tutted. "I'll have to go out **then,** *won't I."*

"Will you set an alarm on your phone when it's time to go and pick her up?"

"What the hell do you take me for? Like I'd forget to pick up my own daughter."

"Well, you don't seem to have remembered to wash her recently, or change her clothes, or brush her teeth and hair. What if you get a migraine so bad that you fall asleep and she's left waiting at the school for you?"

How could Danika say she was worried The Organiser might snatch Amelia from school before Kenzie got there? How could she say that if she wasn't careful, the social services weren't the only people she needed to worry about, someone else waited in the wings to take Amelia away. What kind of shit state would Kenzie get into then? If she was barely coping now, she'd be a right mess if Amelia was kidnapped.

Uncharitably, Danika thought that might actually be the best thing for Kenzie, to wake her up and pull her out of her self-pity pit. But that was a horrible thing to think, especially because Amelia would be frightened with a stranger. But would she? She'd been so apathetic recently, maybe she'd just accept going off with someone she didn't know.

And that was scarier than anything else.

Chapter Twelve

Cameron wasn't a fan of looking down at a little girl who stared up at him and clearly didn't think it was a problem he had a Covid mask on. She'd seemed a bit lethargic of mind when they'd first collected her and hadn't acted bothered when he'd carried her out of the loft room and then the house. She'd been good and kept quiet like he'd told her to, and he found that odd, considering he was a masked stranger. He'd expected her to fight him, to scream, to cry for her mummy. There had been none of that, and even now, she displayed no signs of distress.

Had she been drugged?

He smiled then realised she wouldn't see it. "I'm sorry we have masks on and this might all be a bit scary, but we need to be careful. We don't want you to tell the police that we're bad men when we *saved* you from the bad man. We only need to stay here for a little while, and then we can take you home to your mummy."

"It's okay, there's another man who comes to our house with a mask on."

Cameron, alarmed by what she'd said, frowned and glanced across at Will. He sat on the sofa, trying to act casual while she was on the floor with a Barbie. "What man's that then?"

"He says it's a secret."

Cameron's stomach rolled over. He suspected those words wouldn't mean the same thing if he said them to her. He needed her to keep himself and Will a secret, but he wouldn't be able to word it like that now. "Why does it need to be a secret?"

"Because he said people would be cross if they found out he was there. He comes in when it's dark and Mummy's fast asleep from her tablets."

"What does he do?" He didn't want an answer, not really, but he'd had to ask so he could pass any information to the twins.

"Cuddles and stuff."

He felt bad for being relieved she hadn't gone into detail. "Do you know his name?"

"Matty."

"That's a nice name." He didn't want her to be alarmed, so he'd make out he didn't think there was anything wrong, but alarm bells blared. "How old is Matty?"

"Dunno."

Cameron took his phone out. "I'm going to go and get you a drink. What would you like?"

"The man at the house gave me boxes of juice. I like those."

"Okay, I'll see if we have any."

He left the room, his unease turning to nausea. He accessed the message option and, despite the twins likely being busy with the man from the house, he felt they needed to know this information immediately. Matty could be connected to him.

CAMERON: GIRL TALKING. POSSIBLE PAEDO IN THE MIX. BLOKE CALLED MATTY. GOES TO HER HOUSE AT NIGHT WHEN MOTHER IS ASLEEP. HE WEARS A MASK. CUDDLES HER AND 'STUFF'. I WON'T PUSH HER ON IT BUT WILL LET YOU KNOW IF SHE SAYS ANYTHING ELSE.

GG: WE HAVE AN IDEA WHO THAT IS. SHIT, THIS IS GETTING MESSIER BY THE MINUTE.

If George and Greg already had an inkling, then Cameron could rest easier knowing they'd get to the bottom of this crap. He found some orange juice cartons and took one into the living room, taking the straw out of the plastic wrapper, poking it into the box, then handing the drink to her.

She took it and smiled.

"Do you need anything to eat?" he asked.

She shook her head. "The man gave me a sandwich and a biscuit with chocolate bits in it. I didn't feel sleepy after the sandwich this time, but other times I did."

So she *had* been drugged. *That fucking bastard...*

Cameron looked at Will whose expression above the mask showed exactly what he thought about the situation—if they hadn't both been tasked with babysitting the kid, they'd be out there, searching for this Matty then doing him all kinds of damage. Cameron shook his head, conveying that they had to remain calm and not let their disgust and anger show.

He wanted to reach out and stroke her hair in a fatherly way but couldn't. It would maybe remind her of Matty, and who knew how traumatic that was for her. Plus he'd feel like a paedo himself, even though his concern for her was genuine and he only wanted to comfort her. *Fuck's sake*. "What did you do at the house?"

"I played with Barbie and went to sleep."

"What did the man do?"

"He sat with me sometimes, but he went out a lot because I heard him shut the front door, same as when Matty comes."

Unbidden images entered his head, ones he didn't want.

Amelia lying in the dark after Matty had done 'stuff'.

Amelia crying and in pain.

Amelia not even knowing that what Matty did was so fucking wrong.

Her mother must have been dead to the world if she didn't wake up hearing the front door closing. How was Matty getting into the house?

Christ, was the child letting him in? Had he groomed her *that* much? Was he someone her mother knew? What did he say to Amelia in order to keep her from telling her mum what was going on?

Or does the mum know?

Cameron shut those intrusive thoughts down. He couldn't handle them. He had a daughter of his own, and the thought of something like this happening to her when she was older made him feel sick. Rosie was only a baby at the moment, but she was defenceless, just like Amelia. Vulnerable. The twins had better find this Matty cunt, because if they didn't, Cameron would.

She fiddled with the Barbie's dress. "All her clothes, we forgot them. And her shoes and bags."

"It's okay, maybe you'll get a parcel from the postman with new things for your dolly." *I'll fucking make sure you do.* "You might even get a Barbie house. What about that?"

"She'd like a house."

"It won't have a key for the door, though. Does Matty have a key?"

"He's got a special gold one, he showed it to me."

Cameron's mind was so full at the moment. He wanted to explore the Matty angle but at the same time there was her kidnapper to talk about, too, and how she'd got to Piper Avenue.

"You know the man at the house?" he said.

"Yeah…"

"Is he friends with Matty?"

"I dunno."

"What happened? How did he get you out of *your* house?"

She shrugged. "I just woke up in that bedroom with the Barbie."

"Did he tell you why you were there?"

"He said I had to be a good girl and then I could go home. Matty says I have to be a good girl and then I can go to sleep. I kept waiting for the man to do stuff like Matty but he didn't do nuffin' like that."

Sickened by what he was hearing, not to mention by the images parading around his head, Cameron sat on the sofa, wishing he was anywhere but here. On one hand, he had the burning desire to find Matty and kill him, but before that, he'd talk to him and find out if there were any other children he'd touched. But on the other hand, and selfish as it sounded, he wanted to go home to Janine and Rosie, to where the air was clean and untainted by filth. He wanted to walk away and leave this horror to the twins.

"Do you know how to play Snap?" Will asked her.

He must have realised Cameron was struggling. Cameron gave him a nod of thanks and went into the kitchen for a breather. He rooted around in the fridge and cupboard, finding a tin of beans and sausages. It had been the comfort food of his childhood, so he heated it up and lowered his mask and leaned against the worktop, eating out of the saucepan, itchy from the knowledge he'd gained; he didn't feel comfortable in his own skin; he didn't understand how some men could treat children the way they did. Those fuckers weren't wired right.

His mind drifted to Janine and how she'd suffered at the hands of two men and a woman who'd used and abused her while incarcerating her in a basement flat. She'd taught herself to cope with it, and she'd had therapy, and to anyone else she'd seem the type of woman who had her shit together and nothing bothered her. But the scars were too deep to get rid of, and she battled sometimes to cope with her feelings. Would Amelia eventually get over this, or would it follow her throughout life?

With a cup of coffee in front of him, he sat at the table, listening to her laughing after she'd shouted, "Snap!" To be honest, when he'd first seen her, he hadn't thought he'd hear her laugh—she'd seemed too out of it—but whatever drugs she'd been given must be wearing off; she was at least sounding like a normal kid now.

What worried him most was the fact she wasn't bothered that two men in masks had brought her to another strange house. Was it because she was used to Matty in a mask? Did her mother have men parading through the house so she was used to it? Had she grown up accepting the sight of strangers?

He took a sip of his coffee and messaged Janine.

CAMERON: UNDER WHAT CIRCUMSTANCES WOULD THE POLICE KEEP IT QUIET THAT A FOUR-YEAR-OLD CHILD HAD BEEN ABDUCTED?

JANINE: HELLO TO YOU, TOO.

CAMERON: SORRY FOR JUST DIVING IN, BUT I'M ON A JOB THAT'S FUCKING WITH MY HEAD.

Janine: Shit. Right, it would depend what type of case it was, how sensitive. There's actually a lot of reasons. Why?

Cameron: I'll ring you.

He got up and shut the door, then returned to the table and gave Janine a call, telling her about Amelia.

Janine sighed. "Poor little thing. I wonder what kind of mother she has. I hope she's not like mine."

"No idea. I'm going to have to speak to the twins to see whether it's advisable she even goes home. She might need dropping off at the police station instead."

"A family liaison officer would have already worked out whether the home is unstable. They're trained to spot it. The mother won't even realise she's being observed for certain things. The girl wouldn't be allowed to stay there if there's any doubt she's not safe, so you don't need to worry about that. Even if she's dropped off at home—I assume you're looking after her at the moment?—she could just as quickly be taken to hospital and then put with foster parents while the investigation continued into her home life. But from what you said about this Matty fella, she's likely being abused and her mother has no idea—or the mother takes the tablets so she can pretend she has no idea."

His stomach churned. "That's fucking gross."

"But people do it, love. There are some evil bastards in the world, and mothers aren't immune to being bad. Oh bugger, I'd better go, Rosie's stirring."

"See you later. I hope you manage to get some sleep."

He ended the call and smiled, thankful for the small reprieve where he thought about his daughter instead of someone else's. Janine had worried she would be a shit mum, but she was the best. As for Amelia's… If she *did* know what was going on with Matty, then she was either sick in the head or brainwashed into thinking it was okay.

Not knowing all the answers always did his head in, but in this situation, the frustration of not finding Matty and beating the shit out of him was even worse. He could outright go and ask Amelia the ins and outs, but he couldn't be responsible for traumatising her. While she seemed happy enough and had accepted Matty's visits as normal, there would come a day when she realised it was far from that. He hoped she received therapy to teach her that what Matty did was not okay, and he could only hope that as an adult, she didn't beat herself up about it. Or worse, blame herself.

He put the mask on and went back into the living room and found Will sitting on the floor with her, the pair of them setting up Playmobil—there was a camper van, a small house, and lots of little people, trees, and a Noah's Ark, complete with animals. Cameron could tell Will was good with kids just from watching how he interacted with her—he had a calmness about him that she clearly trusted.

While Cameron was glad she'd taken to Will and himself, it was disturbing at the same time. He didn't think he would ever get over the way the little girl just accepted them bringing her here. She displayed no signs of being afraid, and he found that odd.

What the fuck kind of world had she been brought up in?

Chapter Thirteen

When George had said they might have to take Danika to the cottage, she'd absolutely shit herself. Thankfully, they'd received news that Amelia was in the house, proving Danika wasn't lying. They'd dropped Danika off at home, and she'd been paranoid an undercover policeman sat in a car, watching. The officers at Kenzie's had told her they didn't think she had anything to do with Amelia's abduction, but what if they were lying? What if they'd seen her getting out of a taxi, two men inside with long hair and beards? What if, any moment now, there'd be a knock on the door and they asked her where she'd been and who the men were? She could imagine it now:

"Are those men involved with Ameilia's abduction?"

"Did one of them take her and put her in a van?"

"What's your part in this?"

"Have you put your sister through trauma on purpose?"

"Do you hold a grudge against her because of what went on in your childhood?"

She wanted to scream.

She moved to her living room window and pulled the curtain across a little so she could look outside. She studied the street—the twins' man in the red car wasn't there, so perhaps he was involved in freeing Amelia from Piper Avenue. As far as she could see, no one else was outside, either in a car or standing in the shadows. It didn't mean they weren't, though. The police would have been taught how to keep themselves shielded while on surveillance.

Her nerves seemed to scrape against her insides.

She had the urge to phone Kenzie, but she'd likely be fast asleep having taken a tablet. Ellie might be staying the night, and she could answer the phone. Okay, it wasn't a weird thing that Danika would be phoning her sister to see how she was, but she wasn't sure she could trust herself not to slip up.

George had told her The Organiser had been apprehended. She imagined him chopping the man's dick off like he had with Joseph, torturing him so he got to the truth. Would The Organiser give it to him, though? Would he tell them about Purple? When explaining everything to the twins, she'd felt so ridiculous calling the unknown person by the name of a colour, convincing herself that they thought she was making it up. And she'd been hurt by George's dismissive attitude towards her when she'd asked what would happen to her now. She understood his main concern was Amelia and was grateful that was his priority, but surely he understood how much she'd worry about what they planned to do to her after everything had been sorted out.

She'd mentioned her father's abuse on purpose, to get them to realise she'd been through so much trauma and didn't deserve to have her face cut. They might not think that way, though. She'd kept so much from them, using them to get rid of Farah and Joseph, but surely they must see she was desperate. She could only hope that after they'd spoken to The Organiser, they'd realise she hadn't had any choice. Would they question why she hadn't contacted them as soon as Amelia had been kidnapped? Would they think she was wicked letting her niece go with a stranger?

She made a coffee and sat at the table, toying with her phone, swinging between ringing Kenzie and leaving her be. But maybe she could ring her to see whether Ellie was there. If she wasn't, then she could let George and Greg know the coast was clear and they could drop Amelia home. She hoped Amelia took to Will. Hoped he played cards with her and made her feel at ease. Or maybe she was asleep.

Maybe she wasn't even alive and they'd kept that information from her.

The thought sent her cold. No, she'd have been told if Amelia had been found dead, wouldn't she? Or were the twins so incensed they were currently going to town on The Organiser, blinded by rage?

She pressed the icon to phone Kenzie.

"Hi." Kenzie didn't sound groggy, so maybe she hadn't taken a tablet, or she had and it hadn't affected her yet.

"Are you okay?" Danika wanted to tell her that Amelia was safe, but how could she when she wasn't sure she was? Plus, she didn't dare reveal anything. She could be in enough trouble with the twins as it was without adding more shit they could blame her for.

"Of course I'm not okay, you stupid cow."

"Sorry."

"No, *I'm* sorry. I knew what you meant but I'm taking my frustration out on you. The police don't seem to be getting anywhere. Ellie just left, and I'm no further forward in knowing where Amelia is. It's like I'm being fobbed off. How can she have disappeared into thin air?"

Danika could have reminded her that The Organiser's van had evaded CCTV at a certain point, but it would be cruel to state the obvious.

As clever as he was, he'd probably checked out camera positions well before the abduction. He knew what he was doing. He'd have ditched the van. Who knew, he might have contacts who were willing to torch it or crush it.

Instead, she said, "So Ellie isn't staying tonight?"

"No, but they've got someone posted outside in a car."

Shit. "That's good then. At least you can go to sleep feeling safe."

"I doubt very much her kidnapper would come back for me. Why would he? All he wanted was my baby." Kenzie let out a sob. "Sorry, I keep thinking about paedophiles. I can't get it out of my head."

"You know why that is."

"What if Dad's lying to the police and he arranged this? Or if he found out where we live and he took her to punish me. To punish us. To show us that he's still in control, even though we left home years ago. The type of people he probably hangs around with would be willing to lie about his alibi. And as for Mum… She's a piece of shit who'd lie for him, too. She took his word over ours, don't forget."

"She did." *The bitch.*

"I realised what a cow I've been to my own child. I let myself wallow in what Dad did and didn't even think how it'd be affecting Amelia. I've been worrying about her going to school, about being out in the world, having men as teachers. Men who could abuse her."

"It's unlikely that would happen to her, though. She needs to live a normal life."

"I know, but it's going to be so hard to let her go. We've been on our own all this time. I've shielded her from everything."

"But keeping her indoors is unhealthy."

"I know that," Kenzie snapped, "but I thought it was for the best. When I get her back, things are going to change." She paused, her breathing heavy. "I…" She paused again. "I've done things I shouldn't have to keep her docile."

Danika's stomach rolled over. She knew damn well what she was saying but needed her to admit it. "What do you mean?"

"You must have seen the way she just plays on the floor and doesn't speak much."

"Yes, but what are you actually trying to tell me?"

"It doesn't matter. I'm going to stop it now — stop everything. I'm going to get off my tablets, ask the doctor to reduce the dose until I'm not on them anymore. I let what Dad did to us ruin her life, too. I'm allowing him to control what I do even now."

Danika was desperate for Kenzie to see that what she did by sleeping with men was no different to what Kenzie had done, just in a different way. It probably wasn't the right time to bring it up, but… "Did you have a baby for someone to love?"

Kenzie sniffled. "Yes, but I didn't exactly love her properly, did I? If I was a good mum, I wouldn't have done half the things I've done."

"What did you do?" Although Danika knew. The word *docile* had given it away. But she didn't want to think about that. It was too much on top of all the other crap going on.

When Amelia was returned, she'd probably be taken to hospital, checked over. Would there be evidence of drugs in her system? None from if Kenzie had administered them, too much time had passed, hadn't it? But they might find it if The Organiser had given her some. At least then if Kenzie had been dosing her up regularly, the kidnapper would get the blame. No one ever needed to know it was something Kenzie had done, too.

Danika sighed. Their lives seemed to continually be full of secrets.

"I'm not telling you anything," Kenzie said. "Just know that it stops now. I'm going to be the best mum. Amelia is going to go to school and be a normal little girl. I'm going to therapy to sort my head out."

"The Brothers offer that service. They told me when they took over the Lantern. You don't have to pay for it or anything."

"Then I'll do that. It saves the authorities knowing our business."

"I've spoken to the twins," Danika said, wincing about what she was going to say next. "I told them about Dad. I asked them to kill him."

"Jesus Christ. Won't that fuck things up on the back of what's going on with Amelia? When the police find out he's dead, they might look at us two. They could think we thought he'd abducted her and we got our own back."

"Not if we're always careful about what we're doing. We'll have alibis. It'll be okay. With him gone, we might be able to move on."

"No, we won't, because Mum will still be alive. I'd like to kill her myself for turning her back on us."

"Maybe the twins will let you."

"But then that fucks up my alibi."

Danika rubbed her forehead. "What if I ask them to make them go missing? To kill them and hide the bodies, then empty their house as if they've moved away?"

"But if they're dead they won't be using their bank cards, and that might get noticed. One of Dad's mates is bound to wonder where he is and report him missing. I swear to God he's part of a paedo ring."

"Don't say that."

"You can't tell me you haven't thought about it."

"Of course I have, but... Look, George and Greg will deal with it. They won't do it so we're in the frame."

"I know I've always said I wanted to kill Mum and Dad, but I'd never have done it. Now it's on the table, I'm not sure that's what I want."

"But you just said you'd like to kill Mum."

Kenzie let out a strangled noise. "Just shut up, okay? I've got too much on my mind already without thinking about murdering them."

"Sorry."

"I'm feeling sleepy now."

"Did you take a tablet?"

"Yeah."

"Go to bed then. Everything might look better in the morning."

"I can't see how when the police don't know their arse from their elbow. I keep thinking I'm never going to get her back."

"I've said this before, but we have to keep hoping. She *will* come home, and everything *will* be all right."

"I only wish I could believe you. Night."

"Night."

Danika put her phone on the table and rested her face in her hands. Kenzie was right, there was too much on both their minds, but thank God her sister didn't realise just how much Danika was coping with. Every time she spoke to her, the guilt piled on even more. If only The Organiser hadn't chosen her. He'd told her it was because she had class and was the only woman he'd found who could fit in at the escort agency. If she'd just been a regular sex worker, he would have passed her by and Amelia would still be at home. But she supposed there was a bright side. Amelia being kidnapped had forced Kenzie into taking a long hard look at herself. Danika could only hope that Ellie didn't file a report that Kenzie was an unfit mother, one hooked on antidepressants. If the police decided that Amelia couldn't go back to her mother, Danika dreaded to think what Kenzie would do.

The phone bleeped, and she snatched it up. A message had come through from the twins.

GG: Just putting your mind at rest again that she's safe. Possible delivery to her mother later. Dealing with that arsehole in about ten minutes.

Goddess: I've just spoken to Kenzie. The family liaison officer isn't there, but there's an officer outside in a car. Kenzie has taken a sedative and going to bed.

GG: Good info. Go to bed yourself.

She deleted the messages and pushed up from the table. She went for a shower, flooded with guilt once again that she was so relieved to not be the one dealing with all the crap anymore. There was something to be said about handing your problems over to someone else, someone more capable. Someone who didn't give a shit about the law and got the job done no matter what.

As the water pounded her head, thoughts of Purple came to mind. Would they come for her before the twins found out who they were? Would Oaklynn find her dead body, traumatised for life by the discovery? The ripple effect was real, people touched by other people's actions and decisions. She'd been touched by someone called Purple wanting to take over the sex industry because they were greedy and wanted all the money for themselves. She'd been living her life as best she could, then The Organiser had revealed he'd been paid to do what Purple wanted and he'd chosen her to help him do it.

She was sick of men calling the shots.

She put her hair in a towel turban and dried herself, going into her bedroom to put on some pyjamas. Even though things were still upside down, would she sleep better tonight knowing The Organiser couldn't hurt her and Kenzie? Couldn't hurt Amelia? Was it selfish of her to wish that come tomorrow, everything would have been sorted? Amelia would be home, Kenzie would be allowed to keep her, The

Organiser and Purple would be dead, and the twins made plans to kill her parents.

Kenzie had a point. The police *could* look at the daughters for the murder of their mum and dad, but Danika would stick by what she'd said and ask George and Greg to make them go missing. Maybe it would work out that the police thought Mum and Dad had kidnapped Amelia, and because things had got too hot with the police involvement, they'd returned her and done a runner. In an ideal world, that scenario would be perfect, but as Danika knew all too well, luck had never been on her side, so she braced herself for another shitstorm.

Chapter Fourteen

"I warned you what would happen if you didn't do as you were told." The Organiser's breath hit the back of Danika's ear. He'd approached her from behind and now stood so close his body heat seeped through her thin jacket.

She flinched, wondering what he'd meant. Was he here to hurt her? Had Purple told him she was a lost cause, a waste of time, so had to be eliminated?

"If your sister wasn't so off her tits on her tablets, a certain job earlier on wouldn't have been so easy."

Dread pooled in Danika's stomach. Dare she ask what he was referring to? She had an awful idea of what he'd done, that he'd made good on his promise, but she didn't want to face it. Could she cope with any more shit at the moment?

She dipped her head. "I've told you it's too difficult to ruin the agency and warehouse. I'm doing my best, but there are too many customers being sent there from the Lantern. I told you what Farah expected me to do."

"And I told you, you should be giving them my phone number instead so I can send them Purple's way."

"If I don't do what she wants, Joseph will slash my face and maybe kill me."

"If you don't do what I want, I'll kill you. Anyway, we've gone off topic. I have Amelia."

Danika's whole body went cold. "Oh no. Please, no…"

Her mind raced. Why hadn't Kenzie phoned her? How the hell was Danika going to act in front of the police when she'd known this was going to happen?

They were going to read the guilt all over her face and guess she'd had something to do with it.

"Where have you taken her?" she asked.

He laughed. "You know me well enough by now to realise I'm not going to tell you that. Why would I let you know where my biggest asset is? You're such a thick bitch sometimes. All I'll tell you is she's safe"

"Is she on her own? You're here, so who's looking after her?"

"Again, not something you need to know. Now listen to me. You're going to go to your sister's house. The front door is open slightly, and it's going to worry you, so you'll walk inside. You're going to find Kenzie in the same state as she was when I went into the house, and you're going to search for Amelia. When you can't find her, you're going to run back to your sister and try to wake her up. You're going to have to persuade her to keep Amelia's abduction quiet without telling her why."

"What if I can't get her to do that? She's headstrong. She'll phone the police. And what am I supposed to say? If I'm not allowed to tell her why Amelia was taken, she's going to ring the police anyway because it'll be obvious I've had something to do with it. If I get arrested, I can't help you with the

Lantern, and The Angel, and Kitchen Street, and any other fucking thing you dream up."

He clapped a hand on her shoulder. "Shit."

"That's not like you," she said, smug, "to not have everything worked out beforehand."

He dug his fingertips into her. "I wouldn't be so cocky if I were you. Don't speak, I need to think for a minute."

She stared at the street he'd apprehended her in. Just a normal road with normal houses and cars. If anyone peeked out of their window now, they wouldn't believe the shit she was going through. To some, it might seem odd that a man had his hand on her shoulder, but to others it would just look like a couple standing there talking. And even if they phoned the police, it wasn't like she could admit what she'd been up to, was it.

"Right," he said. "You don't tell her anything. You act as if you've been searching for Amelia in the house and can't find her. Then phone the police and report her missing. You say that the front door was open, so she must have wandered out. I do not want to see it in the papers or online that she's been kidnapped. You need to do your best to say that she left the house on her own."

"Okay. Then what?"

"You act the concerned auntie. Bear in mind the police might watch you to see if you were involved. So you'll need to be careful where you go and what you do."

"So will you. If they see you talking to me, they're going to wonder what's going on."

"Then I'll have to get a bit more creative regarding where I pop up, won't I? Maybe now you'll take me seriously. I want Farah and Joseph dealt with, do you understand?"

"Dealt with?"

"Kill them. Get rid of them."

"What?"

"You heard me. Now this bit stays between me and you. If those jobs don't get done, Purple is going to want the money back that's already been paid to me. It's fifty thousand that I've already spent. There's a ransom demand in the mix now. You pay me fifty grand, and not only can you have Amelia back, you'll be released from ruining the businesses. I've been given another three months to get this shit sorted, and after that, Purple is going to ask for that fifty grand. If you can't find that amount of money, then you know what you have to do. One word about where Amelia is and who took her, and I'm going to kill her."

She nodded and listened to his footsteps as he walked away, remaining where she was until she couldn't hear them anymore. Her mind had blanked out, as if protecting her from the horror of what must have happened this evening. He had Amelia, and if Kenzie needed waking up, he must have drugged her or hit her so she went unconscious. Or had she had her prescription medication upped?

The enormity of everything rushed into her mind and body at the same time. She staggered forward to brace herself with one hand on somebody's brick wall that bordered their front garden. She lowered her backside to it and dipped her head, taking deep breaths. What if any of the neighbours had seen him take Amelia? What if it hadn't even been him and he'd paid some other bastard to do it? What if they'd been rough with Amelia and hurt her? Would they have put cloth in her mouth to stop her from screaming? Had she been asleep and he'd carried her out of the house with no trouble?

Danika wasn't due to start at the Orange Lantern until ten, and if the abduction was about an hour ago, maybe Kenzie and Amelia had been asleep. Maybe Kenzie hadn't even woken up when he'd broken into the house, and she was still out for the count, now, completely unaware her daughter was missing.

She took her phone out and rang the Lantern to say she had a family emergency and could she start work at one a.m. instead. That would give her time to speak to the police with Kenzie. She stood and walked down the street as though calm. She couldn't run in case someone saw her and pointed it out later on once news of Amelia being missing had come out. It was torture not to rush, and half an hour later, she reached Kenzie's street.

The Organiser said he'd left the door ajar, but it was open more than that now. Lots of neighbours were out, including Kenzie, who wandered backwards and forwards across the road outside her house, calling Amelia's name.

It was time for Danika to play her part. She frowned, as though confused about the scene, then grabbed the arm of a passing man. "What's happened?"

"A kiddie has gone missing."

"Who?"

"Little Amelia. Bloody wandered off, didn't she."

"Oh God, that's my niece." She ran towards Kenzie and snatched her into a hug, guilt flooding her system at how much her sister was shaking. She'd done this to her. She'd put her in this pain. She eased back and held Kenzie by the shoulders, asking, "What's going on?"

Kenzie stared at her for a moment, shaking her head as if still unable to believe what had happened. "Amelia... She got the front door open. I woke up, and she was gone... I started my new tablets, and they knocked me out..."

She gave Danika an accusatory glare, as though it was her fault she'd had to take new meds. In a way, it was, because she had *questioned whether the other ones had been working properly. As if she needed more guilt heaped on her.*

"Have you phoned the police?"

Kenzie sighed and looked like she wanted to slap her. "What do you *think? We're all out searching for her while we wait for them to turn up."*

Danika couldn't help but notice that Kenzie wasn't as upset as she should be. Maybe the tablets had dulled her perception of events. Maybe she really did think Amelia had toddled off by herself and she'd be back in a minute. Danika glanced round at everyone else; they appeared frantic and more concerned than her sister.

"What's wrong *with you? You're like a bloody zombie. Your child's missing, for fuck's sake."*

"I just... I just can't get my head around it. Where is she? She knows she shouldn't leave the house without me. Where did she go?"

The tears came then, and Kenzie collapsed onto the road, her face in her hands. She wailed, and Danika couldn't bear it. She almost blurted that Amelia was safe, but she couldn't do that. The Organiser was bound to do something awful to the little girl if he ever found out, and she couldn't have her death on her conscience.

Danika helped Kenzie to her feet and guided her towards her house. Calls of "Amelia!" sounded so mournful and lacked the hope that she'd be found safe. She wasn't sure whether to take Kenzie inside. Would the police bring forensics in to go over the place in case they thought Amelia had been abducted? She led her to the brick garden wall and pushed her down onto it. She took her coat off and put it around Kenzie's shoulders, sitting beside her and drawing her close with an arm around her back.

"What time were the police called?" she asked quietly.

"I don't know, one of the neighbours did it. We'd been out searching for a while when someone said they'd done it."

"Has anyone said whether they'd seen her?"

"No. If I hadn't been asleep... What I did might kill her. What am I going to do then? I can't go to prison."

Danika frowned. "What are you talking about?"

Kenzie whispered, "I gave her a quarter of one of my new tablets."

Danika's anger rose. "What?"

"I... I only wanted her to sleep for a whole night, just for once. She has these nightmares, wakes up, and I'm so tired."

"If she had some of a tablet, how did she get up and walk out of the house?"

"Maybe it didn't affect her as much as I thought it would, because otherwise, that means... It means someone came in and took her."

Aware that it couldn't get in the news that Amelia had been kidnapped, otherwise Danika would pay whatever consequences The Organiser dished out, she leaned closer to Kenzie. "She probably went outside on her own and someone will find her soon. You mustn't mention the tablet, okay? They'll take her away from you for sure. Do you understand?"

Kenzie nodded. "I'm such a shit mother."

Danika wouldn't bother to disagree. They both knew what she felt on the subject, and there was no point in upsetting Kenzie more than she already was. Danika kept her anger to herself about Kenzie drugging Amelia. And it made sense now how The Organiser had been able to take the child out of the *house without her making a sound. She was probably so fast asleep she didn't even know she'd been carried.*

Maybe the tablet should be mentioned. Maybe Kenzie wasn't fit enough to look after Amelia anymore and she'd be better off with someone else. Danika would likely be offered the chance to bring her up, but she wasn't selfless enough to do it. She'd have to get a proper job, a respectable one. It would be too much responsibility. But then Mum and Dad might be asked if she refused, and there was no way she could allow those two to bring up their granddaughter, not with the way Dad was.

Danika felt cruel for not immediately wanting to take the child into her home. That should be the first thing she suggested so Ameila was reared in the right way, but time and again she'd left her with Kenzie, knowing the house was getting in a state and the child might not be fed.

What sort of person does that make me?

She'd chosen not to have children because she wasn't ready and didn't think she ever would be. With her, Amelia might be well fed, clean, and looked after, but mentally and emotionally, she might be no better off. Danika didn't have much she could offer her by way of support and nurturing.

A blue flash of light drew her attention down the road. She stood to peer along the street. The lights stopped flashing, and anyone in the way on the road darted quickly to get on the pavement. The police car came to a stop outside Kenzie's house. Danika approached it, waiting for the officers to get out, then she explained who she was and that her sister was the child's mother.

"Best we talk inside," the policeman said.

Danika took a deep breath and followed them into the house, Kenzie clutching her hand beside her.

Chapter Fifteen

After dropping Danika home, George and Greg had remained in their disguises, sitting in an out-of-the-way lay-by to discuss their next move. Knowing that Will, Cameron, and Ichabod had everything in order, and it would be a while before they were needed at the cottage, they'd sat there hashing things out. Once

Cameron had messaged to say Amelia had been rescued and Ichabod had gone in to collect The Organiser, George had let Danika know the state of play. He still hadn't been sure at that point how they were going to deal with her, but Greg had taken the decision out of his hands.

"If you put yourself in her shoes for just a minute and imagine the fear and pressure she was under, is it any wonder she did things the way she did?"

George had sighed. "I get what you're saying, but there's a voice in the back of my head telling me I've believed people in the past and they've turned out to be liars. That voice comes from you—I seem to recall you drummed it into me to not take people at face value."

"But now you're taking it to extremes."

"You must have known I would, I've got that sort of personality. Listen, I know deep down she's kosher, but there's a part of me that wants to punish her for what she's allowed to happen because a nipper is involved—her *niece*, for fuck's sake. *Family*."

"Take it out on The Organiser and whoever this Purple is, *if* we're lucky enough to find the one who's been pulling all the strings."

They'd discussed taking Amelia home. George was familiar with the street she lived on, and they were the type of neighbours who'd drop everything to help someone in need, so it didn't make sense as to why the abduction had been kept quiet when so many people knew about it. Danika said the residents had all gone out looking for Amelia. With the age of social media and how every aspect of lives were put on show for everyone to see, how come none of them had mentioned the goings-on in the street that night? Why weren't there missing kid flyers on lampposts and SM statuses? Had the police told them to keep it quiet? It infuriated him that he hadn't heard about this. One of their grasses lived on that road, and there hadn't been a peep. He'd be having a word with them when everything died down.

He'd said as much to Greg who'd given one of his usual tuts and shaken his head.

"Think about it this way," he'd said. "If the Old Bill told them that keeping quiet about it might mean Amelia would be brought home sooner, any decent person would go down the route of keeping their gob shut, no matter that we wouldn't be pleased about it. Yes, they know they'll get a bollocking from us, but isn't that preferable to opening their mouths and having a hand in Amelia never coming home? Could you have that on *your* conscience?"

George had accepted that, but he'd still be having a word. "So how are we going to play this?"

"Are you asking me so I feel like I'm involved and you're not making all the decisions, or are you asking me because you haven't got a fucking clue?"

"I've got kind of a clue. We use a stolen car with a dodgy plate and take the kiddie home. We knock on the back door until the mother gets up, then fuck off. But there's the worry that if the residents are that invested in finding whoever kidnapped her, some bastard might be looking out of their window, intent on being the one to be seen as the hero. Yes, we have the fake plates, and yes, we'd be going straight to the scrapyard to get the motor crushed, but they could phone the police and we might not get away quickly enough."

"We can't keep her at the safe house for too long, she's been through enough already, so we need to make a decision pretty soon. In the meantime, we'll go to the cottage and speak to The Organiser."

On the journey there, George had allowed his Mad side to come forward. It didn't take much to get him so angry. Mad was chomping at the bit to get his hands on the man who'd caused so much trouble. He wanted answers and to know who Purple was. This whole story about Purple wanting to take over the sex industry in the East End was fucking ridiculous. There were too many sex workers out there and too many secret brothels for Purple to take over all of them, or at least as Danika had said, take all the custom.

Then that got him thinking about yet another resident who was taking the piss. Purple had been working under the radar. No one, that they knew of, was running a sex racket without their knowledge, so Purple had made the decision to do it on the quiet so he didn't have to pay protection money. That was one of the main rules of the Estate: anyone running a business had to pay up. What was it with people who thought they could flout the rules? It made George think, and not for the first ruddy time, that they were thought of as weak, people who could be run roughshod over, despite the rumours that went round about the punishments they meted out. These chancers had to believe they'd never be caught, that it would never happen to them, otherwise, why take the risk?

They hadn't been at the cottage long when Ichabod had turned up, handing The Organiser over. Apparently, the pleb wanted Purple to be spoken to—that had annoyed George. As if they wouldn't be gunning for Purple anyway. Then to receive a text from Ichabod informing them The Organiser was the little scrote who'd legged it out of Jackpot Palace without paying not too long ago… Upon setting eyes on him, George would have said it wasn't the same man. The gambler at the casino on their internal CCTV had a blond beard with short hair, and this fella was bald and clean-shaven. Had Danika not told them that he must have worn a disguise, he'd have sworn blind they had the wrong bloke.

The fact The Organiser had repaid the fifty grand, leaving it in a bag outside the back of the casino like a coward… It tallied with Danika's story. The Organiser must have paid them with the money Purple had handed over for the jobs. How had he got his hands on the money, though? Had Purple dropped cash off in a holdall or something? Or had it been done via bank transfer, which was dodgy in George's opinion, unless there was a secure way to do it on the dark web. He supposed that was highly likely.

Then Cameron had messaged about this Matty fucker. It wouldn't take a rocket scientist to work out that Matty could be Matthew, Danika's father. That brought its own set of questions. A grandfather abusing his grandchild, yet her mother had cut all ties with him. Or had she secretly kept in contact? Had he still retained control over her and threatened her with all sorts unless she let him fiddle with her kid? If…what was her name, Kenzie? If she was in on this, then she'd find herself at the cottage.

Now he stood in the steel room in full forensic gear, The Organiser naked and hanging from the manacles on the chains attached to the ceiling. He'd cried throughout being stripped and strung up, nothing like the scary man Danika had described to them, but faced with imminent death, many people caved and broke down. His snivelling was getting on George's nerves.

"Shut the fuck up, you noisy bastard." He was sick of calling him The Organiser so asked, "What's your name?"

"Call me Sebastian."

"No, I'll call you by your real name. What is it?"

"Thomas."

"Thomas What?"

"Hughes."

"Right, Thomas Hughes, tell me your story."

It matched Danika's, apart from the fact he'd known Purple way before he'd supposedly made contact on the dark web. And apart from the appalling revelations that had shocked George to his core. He tried to get his head around what had gone on but struggled.

"So Purple is your father."

"Yeah."

"And he contacts you on the dark web to do weird shit."

"Yeah."

"What for? What's the point?"

"So he can control me. I have to tell myself it's a different person, that it isn't him. I pretend I've been sent to do a job. Sometimes he uses a different Organiser, though, to make me jealous, to punish me if I've done something wrong. Like he's saying I'm not good enough so he's picked someone else. The money transfer into my bank is okay because it's from father to son, nothing suspicious or anything. I asked for a loan, you know, to pay you back at the casino, and he told me I'd have to work for it, hence him setting up a job on the dark web and me 'applying' for it. That's what I have to do every time when he bails me out."

"Fucking weirdos, the pair of you. Does he really want to take over the sex industry on our estate, or is that all part of the game?"

"Yeah, he really wants to do that. He's been running women for years, as far back as I can remember. He forced me to have sex with one of them for the first time when I was thirteen."

"With one of his women."

"Yeah."

"As in he's a pimp."

"Yeah."

"Where does your mother fit into all this?"

"She was a prosser. He sent her packing once I was born."

"From what you've told me, I suspect you're a bit fucked up—especially knowing your mother abandoned you." That was an understatement. There was no way this bloke could be completely sane.

"I wish I was someone else. I wish I was Sebastian. He's got his shit together."

"Do you call yourself Sebastian so you can convince yourself you're not Thomas, the bloke who's so spineless he obeys his father, even though what he's instructed to do is wrong?" Harsh of him, but George wanted to make this fucker see that he was pond scum.

Thomas winced.

Mad retreated, leaving George to deal with feelings of sympathy, feelings he didn't want to fucking entertain. From the sound of it, Thomas' life hadn't been the best. He'd been used as a pawn in his father's warped plans. He'd grown up watching women have sex in the family home, punter after punter coming in. He'd kept it quiet, going to school and pretending it wasn't happening. He did whatever he was told despite not wanting to sometimes. Other times he enjoyed it—and George could understand that. He enjoyed hurting people, too. It was the only way he had control when for so long he hadn't had any.

"So why did you pick Danika?"

"It had to be someone who'd fit in at the escort agency. All the other women were just common slags, but she's different."

"Common slags? Are they your father's words or yours?" George glared at him. "Those women are probably trying to get through life as best they can. Your dad sounds a right cunt, and they might not even have a choice about working for him. Did you ever think about that? Does he know you've been using Danika to get the jobs done?"

"No, he'd go fucking mental, but I couldn't do this on my own. He probably knew I couldn't and this was a test. When I told him Farah and Joseph were out of the loop, he assumed I'd killed them, and now he keeps mentioning it, holding it over my head, saying he could ring the police and let them take me away."

"So what happens? You go to his house and talk about this sort of shit over Sunday dinner like it's nothing?"

"No, I haven't spoken to him face to face for years. It's all done on a dark web forum. I have to pretend at all times that he's a client. He doesn't want to see me until I've proved I can be trusted to take over his business when he retires. I know it sounds weird, but I swear, I'm telling the truth."

"Have you told me this in the hope that I'll go easy on you?"

"I just wanted you to know that it wasn't all me, that it was him telling me what to do."

"Like it was you telling Danika what to do."

"Yeah."

"It was bad enough that you'd frightened her and threatened her, that's enough for me to kill you because she's a resident and deserves to live on our Estate in peace." He imagined Greg thinking: *Isn't Thomas a resident who deserves the same, too?* No, he fucking didn't. "But you went a bit too far for me, one step further over the line. You should never have taken the child."

"I know, but Dad was putting pressure on me. He said he'd force me to give him the money back if I didn't get everything sorted quicker, and I couldn't, because I'd paid you back. It took ages for Danika to do anything about Farah and Joseph, and I couldn't risk her taking just as long with the Lantern, so I nicked the kid and… Fucking hell."

"Plus she's also got to fuck up The Angel and Kitchen Street, so I've heard."

"It was her who told you, wasn't it?"

George laughed. "Do you blame her?"

"No. I'd have come to you if I could."

"You make it sound like that wasn't an option when it was."

"If Dad found out…"

"What would he do, kill his own son?"

"So he said, yeah."

"But instead, *I'm* going to kill you, so the outcome ended up the same." George shrugged. While this lad had his mind warped by a bit of a deranged father… "I can't let you walk away from this. You still made decisions of your own, ones your dad didn't put into your head. You chose to kidnap a little girl, and that's something I can't let go of. If you hadn't done that, maybe things would be different. Maybe I wouldn't want to take your testicles out of their sacs and ram them down your throat."

Would Greg fully understand George's earlier dilemma now? Because the girl had been involved, it changed things somewhat, so if Thomas wasn't allowed to get away with it, why should they allow Danika that privilege?

George glanced over at Greg to gauge his thought process, not that he needed to. It seemed his brother had got the gist. Greg nodded, silently telling him they'd think of a fitting punishment for Danika. While she wouldn't die, they'd make sure she never forgot what she'd allowed to happen. If she'd come to them as soon as Thomas had threatened to kidnap the child, things would have taken a different turn. But she hadn't, and here they were. It would be a shame to ruin such a pretty face with a Cheshire, and she was a good asset to the Lantern, so he'd scar her somewhere else, somewhere she'd see it every time she undressed and looked in the mirror.

George nodded back at Greg, message received, and returned his attention to Thomas. "I should feel sorry for you, and I do to a degree, but not enough to let you off the hook. My brother had already contacted our men when you told me what your real name was, but as Hughes is pretty common, we wouldn't want to pick up the wrong Purple, so I'm going to need his first name and address."

"Will you punish him for what he did to me? For what he made me do?"

"Oh yes."

Greg got their phone out and prodded at the screen.

Thomas rotated his head. "And will you tell him it was because of me that you were able to pick him up?"

"If you like. I should imagine it must be nice knowing that you're going to upset him by being the one in control. I can't get it out of my head that you went inside that house and took a sleeping child. You kept her in a loft room and fed her drugged sandwiches. She's a fucking kid, my old son, a *kid*."

Thomas babbled a name and address.

George left the room and went into the kitchen. Greg followed him and made a coffee. They drank it without talking. It might well turn out to be a long old night, but they were going to have to do something about Amelia whether they were busy or not. George couldn't stand the thought of her being parted from her mother any longer than necessary—providing Kenzie hadn't known about Matty being a perv with her kid.

He messaged Will.

GG: How is she?

Will: Asleep. I read her a story.

GG: Softy.

Will: Cameron isn't doing so well. He's struggling that she's probably been abused.

That reminded George to get the ball rolling with regards to Matthew. It annoyed him that he'd been so incensed with Thomas that he'd allowed a paedophile to stay in his bed, oblivious. He told Will to get some sleep and then looked across the table at Greg.

"We need to collect Matthew Cousins. Maybe even the wife."

"Purple will be being picked up, too. We're going to have a full house."

"Come on," George said. "We'll lock that prick in the steel room and go and get Danika's parents."

"Are you going to tell her?"

"Maybe. I haven't decided yet. We'll nip home and get the van."

"Ichabod can collect Purple."

"I assume it was him you contacted to go and check if he's the right Simon Hughes."

"Yep."

George nodded. "Let him know we'll leave a key to the cottage round the back in the rockery, under that big stone. We might not be back in time to let him in."

George got up and turned the light off in the steel room and locked Thomas away. The darkness was an extra punishment, considering Thomas had told them he was afraid of the dark. Cruel to use his weakness against him, but George was past caring. And besides, Mad had told him to do it.

Chapter Sixteen

If his dad was to be believed, Thomas would never amount to much. As a child, he'd watched his dad rule a couple of hundred women, some of them coming to the family home to work with guests of Dad's parties. Thomas had to stay in his little box bedroom when everyone was there, and he had to pee in a Coke bottle instead of leaving the room to go to the toilet. The women would be naked, Dad had said, and the men would have their dicks out.

There had been an unspoken rule that Thomas would never speak about it at school, and besides, he'd been too afraid of his dad to open his mouth anyway. He'd watched him slap women and permanently mark their faces, and once he'd even stabbed a bird in the throat, Thomas watching from the back seat of the car. Dad was the most well-known yet secret pimp around. Ron Cardigan had never suspected him, and neither had the twins.

Thomas scrolled back through one of the previous games, going to the start of the conversation. It wasn't part of the game that he was called The Organiser—he really was one of those but only did small, menial jobs in order to get that title and be allowed onto the dark web forum.

CLIENT: GO TO 54 ARCHIBALD STREET AT EIGHT O'CLOCK TONIGHT AND WAIT FOR THE WOMAN TO LEAVE THE HOUSE. SHE'LL BE USING SHANK'S PONY, SO FOLLOW HER. SHE'LL TURN LEFT, INTO THE PARK, LIKE SHE ALWAYS DOES. GO AFTER HER. JUST BEFORE YOU SLIT HER THROAT, ASK HER WHAT HER NAME IS.

THE ORGANISER: HAVE I BEEN PAID?

CLIENT: I'VE SENT THE 30K OVER. YOU'RE SUCH A USELESS PRICK.

THE ORGANISER: SORRY.

He was always saying sorry, always trying to get on his dad's good side. It had been difficult to grow up under the disparaging eye of a parent who'd said he'd kept his child only because it would upset the slag of a mother. How much must it have hurt for her to walk away, leaving her baby behind? She'd had no choice, Thomas would bet, although Dad hadn't gone into detail about it. Maybe she'd had Thomas and took her opportunity to run. He doubted he'd ever know the truth.

He leaned back and thought about the past.

Fifty-four Archibald Street stood nestled between its red-brick companions as though it defiantly tried to remain standing. The whole row leaned a bit, the houses older than the two world wars. One of the chimneys three doors down had crumbled on one corner, and some of the roof tiles were missing. Each property was skinny, probably two-up, two-downs with only a small concrete yard for a back garden. Each front door butted against the pavement, and someone next door to number fifty-four had clearly tried to brighten things up by having holly in a window box.

Thomas doubted it would last very long. Some kids would come by and pick it.

Thomas stood on the opposite pavement in the mouth of a narrow alley, high, frost-drenched hedges either side of him. He was metres away from a lamppost so stood in relative darkness, watching, waiting. He stamped his feet to keep warm, December bloody cold this year. Christmas Eve was hardly a time to be slitting some poor cow's throat, was it, but it wasn't as if he had a choice.

At eight o'clock, she emerged just like he'd been told she would. Was she going to work or maybe a night out at the pub? She headed across the road towards him. Shit, the alley must lead to the park, but when she reached the other side she continued on ahead of him, her heels clip-clopping, her breath misting in the chilly air. She had a cream-coloured fur hat on and carried on until just before reaching the end of the street, turning into another alley, again with high hedges either side.

He followed her down it towards the blackness at the end. It felt like he was in a maze until he stepped out at the other end. If it wasn't for the hat, he wouldn't be able to see where she'd gone. It bobbed in the darkness with each of her steps, and he took off in pursuit, treading carefully so his boots didn't thud on the grass. He judged she was about halfway across the park now, so if he was going to do as he was told, he'd have to get on with it. He took his flick-knife from his pocket and released the blade, upping his pace.

He was right up behind her in no time, and she must have sensed him because she gasped, then ran ahead, shrieking. He chased her, thumping her in the back of the head. She went sprawling forward, landing on the grass. With his eyes. accustomed to the darkness, he made out her shape. She lay on her side, scrunched in the foetal position with her hands over her head. He got down on his knees and roughly pushed her onto her back, straddling her.

She cried out again, and he cursed not being told to bring a cloth to stuff in her mouth, but then maybe that was the point. He'd been taught to do everything his father said to the letter, yet at the same time, he was being tested to see how he coped with the instructions and whether he was savvy enough to deviate from them when a dilemma presented itself. Thomas had forgotten he was supposed to be showing how competent he would be when running his father's business, but it was so difficult to change his mindset when all he'd heard growing up was to only do what Dad said.

He slapped a hand over her mouth, and so she knew he meant business, he rested the blunt edge of the knife against her throat. "I don't want to do this, but I have to."

She said something beneath his hand, but it was muffled and didn't make any sense. He supposed she was pleading for her life, and he was glad he couldn't hear it. If he did, he might let her go.

"I need you to tell me your name. If I take my hand away, will you promise to say it quietly?"

She nodded so violently it dislodged her hat which went skew-whiff, one edge covering an eye. He slowly peeled one finger up at a time, and at her rapid intake of breath, he knew she was going to scream. He covered her mouth again and pressed the edge of the knife harder.

"I can turn the blade around, you know, so it slices you. Now then, do as you're fucking told or I will, do you understand me?"

She nodded again. He pulled his fingers away again.

She whispered, "Rachel Sebastian."

He jammed his palm back down and blinked at what she'd said. Was this some kind of a sick joke, or did his father really expect him to slit her throat? So many emotions swirled around inside Thomas that he went lightheaded and felt sick. If the abandonment story was true, then he should slice her neck without a second thought, but what if it wasn't?

"You had a baby, didn't you?" He told her the year he'd been born.

She nodded.

"Did you choose to leave him?"

She nodded.

Thomas turned the blade over and cut her skin. At least that was one truth Dad had told him, but that voice in the back of his head whispered that she could have chosen to leave him, but she still may not have wanted to. She could have had no choice. She could have been told that if she didn't go, then Thomas would be killed. It was the kind of sick shit Dad would say.

Stunned and panicking that he'd get caught, he got off her, bending to wipe his knife on her coat. He flipped the blade inside the handle and, glad he had a black jacket on so no blood would be seen, he dropped it in his pocket. He backed away from her, unable to believe he'd killed the one woman he'd been desperate to meet all of his life. He shouldn't have been so impulsive. You should have spoken to her some more.

He turned around in a circle to check the vicinity and left the park the way he'd entered it, finding his car and driving away. He went past fifty-four

Archibald Street and imagined all of her things in there. What were they like? What was her favourite style? Did she have a picture of him in a frame on the mantelpiece? If he went in, would he learn more about her?

He got home and put his clothing in the washing machine, desperate to get some answers from his father.

THE ORGANISER: WHY DIDN'T YOU TELL ME SHE WAS MY MOTHER?

CLIENT: WASN'T IT SO MUCH BETTER TO DISCOVER IT FOR YOURSELF?

Dad was insane, Thomas was sure of it. He hoped he'd learn to stand up to him one day, but how could he when he funded his gambling habit? As soon as Thomas lost big, he went crawling to his father who gave him a job to do to earn the money.

It was so fucked up it wasn't funny.

There's no hope for me. I'm a lost cause.

Chapter Seventeen

It seemed Ichabod had barely got back to Jackpot Palace when he was called out again to go to an address and check the identity of a resident called Simon Hughes. The key to finding out if it was the person the twins wanted was to establish who Simon's son was. Ichabod wondered why the twins hadn't asked Colin, their copper, to look on the database, but considering the time of night, Colin might not be at work, plus if another officer clocked that Simon's name had been looked up, it would alert the police to something going on if Simon happened to go missing.

Ichabod had been instructed to take him to the cottage if he was Thomas' father. He assumed Thomas was The Organiser who must have squealed. It wasn't difficult to imagine the scenario; he was probably naked and hanging from the ceiling in the steel room, all of his dignity gone, his future made clear. Not that he'd have one for long.

Using one of the stolen cars, and with a brown wig and long beard, plus gloves on, he pulled up outside the house. It was a big fecker, would have cost a fortune, not to mention the flash Audi on the driveway. He got out and mentally prepared himself to approach the front door. He was still amped up from breaking into the house and collecting Thomas, so he had enough adrenaline floating in his veins to get him through the next few minutes. The only problem he foresaw was if Simon had a guest. Or a wife. He hadn't been given any information about the bloke so was basically going in blind.

He checked the street for any nosy parkers and, seeing none, turned to assess the house. It was detached with murky alleys down either side and gates that would lead to the back garden. A red light pulsed on an alarm box next to one of the bedroom windows. Was it only a deterrent? There were no CCTV cameras, nor was there a video doorbell, but that didn't mean his movements weren't being tracked.

He walked up the drive and knocked on the door, rolling his shoulders to loosen his muscles in case he had to resort to martial arts. Some people didn't take verbal urging well and needed a little more persuasion. It didn't matter to him what size Simon was; he'd taken down big blokes in his time, and tonight would be no different.

A light to his left flashed on, and the door opened to reveal a skinny man in blue jeans and a white polo top, a fuck-off massive purple birthmark covering the majority of one cheek. Ichabod hid his reaction and smiled.

"Simon Hughes, father of Thomas?"

"Yeah, what of it?"

"Excuse me for just a second." He took his phone out.

ICHABOD: I'VE GOT OUR MAN. WILL BE DELIVERING HIM SHORTLY.

He put the mobile away and smiled at Simon. "I need tae come in for a chat."

Simon frowned then barked laughter. "What the fuck would I let *you* in for? I don't know you from Adam."

"Ye'd let me in because I work for The Brothers."

Simon paled and seemed to contemplate whether he should slam the door or not. He must have seen sense because he stepped back and held a hand out in a gesture that said Ichabod was welcome to come in. Or not welcome, but that he knew he didn't have a choice. Ichabod waited for him to move back farther—he didn't trust that the fella wouldn't lash out the second he entered the property. Seeing he was out of reach enough, Ichabod walked in and kicked the door shut behind him.

"Watch it," Simon groused, "that cost me two grand."

"I have tae be honest and say I don't give a feck. Is anybody else in the house?"

"That would be telling." Simon smirked.

"Are ye seriously goin' tae feck me about when I've told ye I work for the twins?"

Simon folded his arms. "How do I know you're telling the truth?"

"Ye don't. Now answer me, is anyone else in the house?"

Simon shook his head. "No one, unless you count the tart in my bedroom."

"Is she your wife?"

"Is she fuck."

This could be potentially fecking irritating if he had to deal with this prick plus a woman. "Ye're goin' tae go upstairs and get her. I'm goin' tae go wid you."

Simon let out a gusty sigh and turned to walk up the stairs. Ichabod had an uneasy feeling so remained on high alert. He followed him up and into a large bedroom, waiting for Simon to show his hand.

Ichabod glanced around. "Where's the tart?"

Simon spun round, his fists raised. "There isn't one. Now get on the fucking floor on your knees."

Ichabod laughed—the audacity of the eejit. "I don't think so."

He did a roundhouse kick, his foot connecting with the side of Simon's face.

The man went down onto *his* knees, a hand going up to lay flat against his temple. "Fucking hell, was that necessary?"

"It seems it was. Ye apparently think ye're the one callin' the shots." Ichabod took a cable tie out of his pocket and moved round to wrench Simon's hands behind his back. He secured his wrists and hauled him to his feet, no strength needed as he was a weedy little fecker. "Where's ye phone?"

"In my back pocket."

Standing behind him and gripping one twig-like arm, Ichabod took it out. He pressed the button on the side to switch it off then tossed it on the bed. "The Brothers want a word wid ye. I don't rate ye chances much, I doubt ye'll be comin' home again."

"What's this about, me not paying protection money?"

"I have no idea," Ichabod lied, "but seein' as they have ye son, maybe that might give ye a clue as tae what they want."

"What's that stupid little shit done now?"

"That's for the twins tae tell you, or maybe Thomas himself will."

Ichabod led him out of the room and gave him a shove to go down the stairs. He let go of his arm and allowed the man to lead the way. "Go in the kitchen."

Simon obeyed, and Ichabod grabbed a dishcloth from the side of the sink and stuffed it in his mouth. Simon's face reddened, his birthmark turning an even more livid shade of purple. It was raised and lumpy.

He marched him out of the house and into the back of the car, doing the same as he'd done with his son and cable tying his wrists to the handle above the door. He clipped a seat belt over him and took the cloth out of his mouth, then shut the door quickly. He wanted the man to be able to speak to see if he told him any information the twins might need to know. He checked the street again and got in the driver's seat, starting the engine and heading towards the cottage.

"At least tell me what my kid's done," Simon muttered.

"Feck off."

"I'm telling you, whatever it is, it won't be anything to do with me."

"I'm sure that's not true, but ye tell yeself that if it makes ye feel better."

He glanced at Simon in the rearview mirror. The man stared outside, the cogs clearly turning in his mind. He was likely thinking up a story to get himself out of the shit and put his son firmly in it. He seemed the type not to care that he'd be throwing his lad to the wolves.

"He's gone and told them about the game, hasn't he? Or he's got himself caught for killing that couple. What an absolute fucking bellend."

"What couple?"

"The pair who ran the escort agency and those kinky sex parties."

"And why would he do that?"

"Because he's a dickhead. Because he's useless and he couldn't do what I asked him to."

"What did ye ask him?"

"I'm saying nothing."

Ichabod drove on and took the track towards the woods.

"Hang about," Simon spluttered. "Where the fuck are you taking me?"

"Ye'll soon see."

"What are they going to do, kill me in the fucking forest?"

"That would be tellin'."

"But I haven't *done* anything. It's all my son."

"Ye're a nasty piece of work."

"That kid's a fucking liability. I've been trying to get him to prove himself for years, but I should have known he wasn't up for it. Thick as mince."

Ichabod parked outside the cottage and got out of the car. He walked round the back and found the large stone, taking the key from underneath it. He returned to the front and opened the door, then went back to the car and used his flick-knife to cut the cable tie, dragging Simon out and into the cottage. The bloke lost a shoe in the process; *I'll pick that up later*. Ichabod held Simon's arm while he used the other key on the ring to open the door to the steel room. It was dark, so he flicked the light on. As he'd predicted, Thomas hung from the chains. He shoved Simon towards his son and watched his reaction.

"Jesus fucking wept." Simon went over to Thomas and headbutted him in the chin. "You're such a useless piece of shit cunt. What have you told them?"

Thomas smiled. "You'll see."

Ichabod took hold of Simon again and yanked him over into the back corner. He pulled another cable tie from his pocket and secured the man's ankles. He hadn't been told what to do now so assumed he'd have to babysit. He went to sit on a chair next to the tool table and observed how Simon stared daggers at his son's back. The emotions flickering over his face said it all: he hated his boy.

Ichabod's phone chirped, so he checked the message.

GG: IF YOU'VE DROPPED THE MAN OFF, GO TO THE SAFE HOUSE AND COLLECT THE CHILD. ADDRESS TO FOLLOW. A COPPER IS SITTING OUTSIDE IN A CAR, SO YOU'RE GOING TO HAVE TO GO ROUND THE BACK. MAKE SURE HER MOTHER TAKES HER INSIDE. THEN MAKE YOURSELF SCARCE. MORE INSTRUCTIONS TO COME FROM DWAYNE.

It was going to be tricky, returning a kidnapped child to her mammy when a copper was in the vicinity, and although the prospect was daunting, there was no way he'd say no. The girl needed her mother.

"I'll leave you two tae have a little chat."

He left the room and locked them in, retrieved the shoe, threw it into the cottage, then got in the car and drove towards the safe house, praying it would all go without a hitch.

Chapter Eighteen

George and Greg had collected their van and sat outside a row of identical terraced houses, even down to them all having white uPVC doors. He assumed they were owned by the council or a housing association. He had his eye on the one in the middle, number fifteen, all the curtains shut and only one light on downstairs, probably the living room.

"Are we going to announce who we are, because they're not going to recognise us with these beards and wigs, providing they've ever seen us before. I'm actually surprised Thomas didn't question who we are."

Greg chuckled. "He was probably too scared to even think about it, but yes, it'll be quicker if Matthew knows it's us."

"Did I do the right thing with Thomas? He has to die, yes?"

"Yep."

"And I read you right, didn't I, about Danika?"

"She can't just walk away without some form of punishment. We've allowed it to happen before, but because a little girl was involved…"

"Yeah, I get it. And she's her auntie, too, which makes it even worse in my book. She let her sister worry."

"Maybe there's some resentment from their childhood that's playing a part."

"Fuck knows. Come on, let's get this over and done with."

They go out of the van, and Greg unlocked the back doors, leaving them ajar so it would be easier for when they brought the couple outside. George took the lead up the front path, glancing left and right to check for any nosy neighbours, but most of the lights were off and all the curtains were closed. They'd be fucking unlucky if someone spotted them. He tapped on the door quietly, then spotted a doorbell, which prompted him to peer at the doors either side in case they had bells with cameras. None of them did, but there could be some across the street. He felt safe enough in his disguise so pressed the button and waited.

A bloke in a white vest answered, giving George I-beat-my-wife vibes. His stomach protruded so much the shape of his outie belly button was clearly visible beneath the material. Matthew had a bit of beef on him, thick upper arms and meaty fists, but George wasn't fazed.

"Yeah?" Matthew said.

"We might not look how you imagined, but my name is George Wilkes, and this is my brother, Greg."

Matthew gawped. "Oh, for fuck's sake. Have those girls gone and told you I stole Kenzie's little girl?"

"No, we're aware of who did that, but Danika told us something else instead. Something about your hands and dick being in places they shouldn't be."

"What the chuff are you on about? You do know my daughters have got mental health issues, don't you? They make shit up all the time."

A woman came from a doorway to the left, her appearance stopping George's response. She looked afraid, as if she'd been listening and had heard George introduce them. She whittled her skinny fingers then raised one hand to flutter it at her scrawny neck. She stepped closer, standing behind her husband as if for protection.

"What's happened?" she asked.

"The Brothers are here because of those fucking girls, Nina," Matthew said. "They've gone and told them some bullshit story about me."

Nina pinched her bottom lip. "The same one as they told me?"

"Yeah, that one. And we all know what bollocks *that* was." Matthew smiled at George. "Why don't you come in and we can talk about this over a cup of tea?"

George smiled back. "That's very kind of you, don't mind if we do."

They stepped inside and followed the couple into the kitchen that needed a good clean. Plates and cups piled on the worktop, the sink also full of crockery with sauces and remnants of food on them that had dried, days old. Towers of washing covered the dining table, some of them falling over where they must have ferreted for what they wanted to wear and didn't care where the clothes landed. It had the air about it of a woman who'd given up.

Had Nina blocked out the abuse because if she hadn't, she would have broken down? Despite her daughters being touched inappropriately when they were little, was it safer for her to agree with her husband and take his side? Was he handy with his fists? The state of the room said he wasn't the type to force her to keep up with the housework, so perhaps he didn't mind living in a mess. From what Danika had said, he spent a lot of time at the Lock and Key pub, so he'd barely be at home to see it anyway.

Considering the filth, George said, "On second thoughts, don't worry about that cuppa. Why don't you tell us about your girls and their stories."

Matthew seemed pleased he was being believed, but regardless, he folded his arms over his chest, a defensive stance. "Danika told her mother that I'd been fiddling with her sister, that I'd fiddled with her, too, but it wasn't true. Who the fuck touches their kids, eh? I'm not that way inclined, never have been."

"Why do you think she made something like that up?" George asked.

"For attention? Who knows? It almost ruined our marriage, didn't it, Nina?"

His wife nodded. "It was a dreadful time. I couldn't believe she'd say such a thing. Then Kenzie said the same. They must have cooked it up between them."

"How were things at home after that?" Greg asked.

Matthew hugged himself. "Well, it couldn't have been true because they didn't go to the police or anything. If they were that bothered, they'd have wanted me carted down the nick, but they stayed here until they were old enough, then they fucked off without telling us. Charming, that is. You bring them up and put a roof over their head and that's how they repay you."

George hoped his expression showed his fake sympathy; Matthew had just given him an idea of where to steer the conversation. "As it happens, I've got Danika and Kenzie in one of our secret locations. We didn't believe their story either, and we think you've got the right to put your side across, so why don't you come with us and we'll confront them together?"

"What's Kenzie doing at one of your places when her kid's missing?" Matthew asked. "It just shows what kind of mother she is if she's prepared to leave her house when her little girl could turn up at any second. Selfish, that's what she is, always thinking about herself."

"She didn't have any choice," George said. "We were that annoyed we forced them to come with us. We don't like people who tell stories."

Neither of them picked up on his meaning.

Nina plucked at the baggy skin on her neck. "Oh, I don't know, maybe we should leave it. We don't want to go raking up old arguments."

Matthew seemed happy she'd said that.

George raised his eyebrows. "You don't want to clear your name?"

"I bloody do," Matthew said. "Let's see what they've got to say, shall we, when we're standing in front of them. Come on, woman, get your coat and shoes on."

This had gone easier than George had expected. "We've only got our van outside, so you might be a bit uncomfortable in the back."

"We're not bothered about that. We just want to get to the truth." Matthew ambled into the hallway, Nina following.

George cocked an ear, suspecting there were going to be a few whispers.

"What are you doing?" Nina said urgently. "Once they open their mouths, they're not going to believe us."

"You leave it to me."

George and Greg joined them in the hallway, Nina jumping out of her skin while putting her arm into her jacket.

George helped her with the other arm and smiled at her reassuringly. "I just heard what you said, and don't worry, we have ways of getting the truth out of people."

They left the house, the couple getting into the back of the van and sitting on the wheel arches. George and Greg sat in the front, and George glanced across at his brother as if to say, "These two are something else." Greg nodded and fired the engine up, easing out of the parking spot.

"Are you all right back there?" George called.

"It's a bit uncomfortable, but don't you worry about us," Matthew said.

No one spoke on the journey. When they arrived at the cottage, George quickly thought about the logistics, cementing them in his mind. They left the van and let Matthew and Nina out, George leading the way to the front door. Inside, he switched the light on in the hallway and went into the living room, turning on a couple of lamps.

"Ooh, this is nice and cosy," Nina said. "Is this where you live?"

"No, it's somewhere we take people when they've been naughty," George said.

"I'd say our girls have been more than fucking naughty," Matthew muttered.

Nina fussed with her neck again. "What will happen if the police go to Kenzie's and find out she's not there? They might have news about her daughter…"

"I don't particularly give a fuck," George said. "They've lied to us and they need to pay the price."

Matthew smiled smugly and parked his arse on the sofa, getting himself comfortable. "Where are they, then?"

"We've tied them up in one of the bedrooms." Greg moved towards the door. "Shall we talk to them in here or in there?"

Matthew got up. "We'll go in there. I'd like to see them trussed up like chickens. Honestly, the pain they've put us through…"

He was good at pretending, and George could see how his wife had swallowed his story with how he came across as so convincing, but something Nina had said earlier popped into his mind. *Once they open their mouths, they're not going to believe us.*

Us. So was she in on it all along? That she'd stayed with him anyway sickened George. Or had Matthew forced her to stay with him? Had she suspected the abuse but couldn't quite believe it when confronted with the truth? Had he convinced her she'd imagined thinking he was creeping into their children's bedrooms? Where did she think he went when he visited Amelia, or was she asleep and didn't have a clue? So many questions.

Greg left the room, Matthew and Nina following, George taking up the rear. Greg unlocked the steel room door and switched the light on, standing to one side to usher the couple in. George pressed in tight so they couldn't run once they realised their daughters weren't there.

Matthew stared at Thomas, his mouth flapping, then he looked at George. "What's going on?"

Nina caught sight of the occupants of the room and spun round, bumping into George's chest. She pushed at him, screeching, and he gripped her upper arms, giving her a shake.

"Did you honestly think we believed you, you stupid fucking cow? You stayed with a pervert. How did you sleep at night?"

"He threatened me," she said. "I had to stay."

"So you turned your back on your girls rather than get them the help they needed? Some mother you are."

Did Danika have similar traits to her mother? She hadn't got Amelia the help she needed either, letting her be taken. George had some of his father's traits, which he hated, but at least he tried to stop them from appearing.

George locked the door. Greg shoved Matthew against the wall and grabbed a cable tie off the tool table. He yanked his arms behind him and tied his wrists, then plonked him on the chair. "Sit there and don't move."

Matthew eyed the tools.

Greg glared at him. "You just try it." He pushed the tools to the farthest end of the table, out of the way.

Nina continued to battle George who was getting a bit pissed off. He twisted her so her back faced him and marched her into the opposite corner where he caught his first sight of Simon Hughes. The man sat on the floor and leaned against the wall, snivelling, and his name now made perfect sense. He had a purple birthmark covering his cheek.

"Sorry, I haven't had a chance to introduce us yet," George said to him. "What a bad host I am. I'm George, and that's my brother, Greg."

He pushed Nina to her arse on the floor, holding a hand out for Greg to give him cable ties. Greg had already read his mind and passed them over. George sorted her wrists and ankles, scrunching his nose up at a dark stain marking her jeans.

Why do people insist on pissing themselves?

He left her to it and went to stand next to Matthew in front of Thomas. He dressed in a forensic suit and gloves, Greg doing the same, hoping it made a nice point that they didn't want to get their suits dirty, that blood would be shed.

"That's where you're going to end up," George said to Matthew and gestured to the chains. "But first I need to deal with him before I can put you up there."

He picked up his current favourite weapon, a sword, and drove it into Thomas' stomach. He left it in there and glanced down at Matthew who shook and blubbered nonsense.

"Sorry, I didn't quite catch that." George smiled. "Are you telling me you don't want me to do that to you? Well, tough shit." He withdrew the sword and got to work hacking at Thomas' body.

Thomas screamed, and Nina joined him. Simon shouted out, "Oh my God!" and Greg told him to shut his face. George cut and sliced, creating ribbons of flesh, eviscerating a patch of stomach to the point intestines poked out. George reached out and grabbed them, the innards slippery against his gloved fingers and palm. He wrenched, revelling in Thomas' scream that quickly grew silent. The body went limp, and blood pissed from the wounds down his legs, dripping off his toes onto the trapdoor. Nina sobbed, her eyes closed, and George would bet she wished she'd grassed her husband up years ago, but it was too late and she had to face the consequences.

He glanced at Simon who appeared horrified, but not horrified enough. George twisted Thomas' body so his father got a better view of the mess George had made.

"This is your fault," George said. "You made your boy do all those things. You made him die. If only he hadn't kidnapped that little girl…"

Simon's eyes widened. "What? What little girl?"

George believed him; his reaction had been so genuine. He filled him in on what Thomas had done, hammering it home that if Simon hadn't played the games on the dark web, none of this would be happening. He stalked over to the corner and speared the sword into Simon's mouth, downwards, driving it in hard until the tip whacked into the wall. There was slight resistance where he imagined the metal had pierced the top of the spine. Blood gushed from between Thomas' lips and crept out of his ears. Nina screamed, her eyes scrunched closed so tight her crow's feet were more pronounced, tears coasting down her cheeks. The sound of heaving from behind came from Matthew.

Greg barked, "Get a grip and grow a pair."

George left the sword where it was; Simon could die slowly and painfully for all he cared. He stalked over to Nina and gripped her coat, hoisting her up to her feet. "There's a special place in Hell for people like you. The secret keepers. The ones who condone what their husbands have done or turn a blind eye. No matter what he did to you, you should have stepped up to the plate and saved your girls, but you didn't. God only knows what your actions did to them, how hurt they were that you turned your back on them, the one woman who was supposed to believe them above all others. You don't deserve to be called a mum."

He shoved her so she fell to the floor and banged her head on the wall. She cried out, shaking, probably trying to come to terms with her evening turning to shit so quickly.

George looked at Greg. "I've had enough for now. We'll come back to these two later."

He cleaned himself down using the hose on the wall, having to rinse blood from his beard, opened the trap door, and released Thomas from his manacles, letting him fall into the hole beneath. He glanced over to check the state of Simon who appeared to have carked it, the blood flow from his mouth slower. Beside the door, George took his outfit off and dropped it on the floor. He exited, tired, leaving Greg to lock up. In the kitchen, he got on with making coffee and taking some ready meals out of the freezer. He was starving hungry.

Greg joined him and sat at the table. "I bet there's going to be a conversation going on in there."

"Yeah, lots of blame bandied about. I wouldn't put it past Matthew to convince her he's innocent even now. I'm not sure how we're going to do this. What if Danika wants to see her parents die? How are we going to get around that when she needs an alibi if Kenzie rings her to say Amelia's home? She'll be expected to go and see her or it'll look well iffy."

"We can go and get her in a few. We'll rope her neighbour into saying they were together."

George nodded, watching his tuna pasta bake going around and around in the microwave. He took some garlic bread out of the freezer and popped it in the Ninja, wishing he had his go-to food instead. He needed comforting, but he hadn't restocked on Pot Noodles for this place.

"We'll go to the shop in the morning," Greg said.

George nodded, unsurprised his brother knew what he was thinking.

Chapter Nineteen

The tension was rife in Kenzie's house. PC McFarlane, a brown-haired man in his thirties, had immediately looked around the house. The other officer, PC Cheryl Croft, had gone into the living room with Danika and Kenzie. Other officers had turned up to search the garden, the shed, and the loft. Danika presumed others were in the street and the *surrounding area. She imagined they'd be knocking on doors to see if someone had taken Amelia inside, not knowing where she lived—but who would do that and not phone the police? Kenzie had already been through the evening's events twice, Cheryl writing it down then going over and over it so Kenzie could add bits that she may have forgotten. Now it was Danika's turn.*

"Did Kenzie phone you to let you know Amelia had gone missing, which is why you're here?" Cheryl asked.

"No, I was on my way for a visit and realised something was wrong when I saw everybody out in the street."

"Is it usual for you to visit without asking then?"

"Well, yes, she's my sister... I'm here a lot."

"Any set schedule?"

"No, just as and when I've got the time to turn up. It just so happened I chose tonight."

"Where were you prior to your arrival here?"

"At home. I had dinner with my next-door neighbour, Oaklynn. She's a widow, so we eat together every so often because she gets lonely."

Kenzie gave Danika a filthy look, as if she wasn't allowed to have friends or spend time with anyone other than her.

Cheryl smiled. "And where is it you live?"

Danika gave her address. Thank goodness she'd actually been with Oaklynn and she had an alibi if the police went down the abduction route. It hadn't been mentioned so far, so maybe they were still going with the idea that Amelia had left the house on her own.

Cheryl switched her attention back to Kenzie. "And what about Amelia's father? Where is he?"

Kenzie blushed. "I actually don't know who he is. It was one of two so…"

"Did either of them know they could be the father?"

"I never told them I was pregnant, so no."

"So you don't think that either of them would have come here to take Amelia?"

"How could they if they don't know she exists? And anyway, how did they get in? They'd have had to break in, and there's no glass on the floor or anything like that."

"You said the front door was open when you woke up." Cheryl paused. "How tall is Amelia?"

This was the kind of thing that was going to trip them up. The police had to be specialised in these types of cases, surely, so they'd definitely wonder whether a four-year-old could reach the Yale lock.

"I don't know," Kenzie said but held her hand up to estimate the height. "If you're asking to see whether

she can open the door by herself, yes, she can. She's tall for her age."

"What time did Ameila fall asleep?"

"About seven."

"And yourself?"

"I've already told you, half past."

"And you woke up when?"

"Nine."

"That's great, that all matches."

"Of course it does," Kenzie snapped, "because I'm telling the truth."

Cheryl took Kenzie's testy response in her stride. "Where did Amelia go to sleep?"

Kenzie looked like she wanted to scream. "On the armchair. I was on the sofa. Look, I've said this already."

"Sorry, I'm just trying to cement the scene in my head, that she woke on the chair, left the living room, and decided to open the front door. I don't understand why she'd do that if you were on the sofa. If she didn't need to look for you, why go outside?"

"I don't know."

"Have you ever left her in the evening?"

"No!"

"In the daytime?"

"No."

"So there would be no reason for her to have not seen you under your blanket and panicked, thinking she'd been left?"

Danika couldn't sit by and listen to this without saying something. "My sister and niece are always together. Kenzie wouldn't dare leave her alone."

"How do you know if you don't live here?" Cheryl smiled. "I'm not deliberately being mean. These are the sorts of questions that will be asked later down the line if Amelia doesn't turn up."

"Why? Because it'll be assumed she's been abducted?" Danika asked.

"Or unfortunately, that you, Kenzie, have done something to her." Cheryl quickly raised a hand. "I'm not suggesting that at all, but these are scenarios we have to look into."

"I understand," Kenzie said. "I just want her to be found. Like I said earlier, I'm wondering if she's gone to the park or the little shop. They're both places we go to regularly. Or we did—until I got poorly anyway."

Danika could have slapped her.

"Poorly?" Cheryl queried.

"Well, not poorly, it's just I'm on anti-depressants. I've been finding it a bit hard to cope."

Danika was worried they may think Kenzie had neglected Amelia. This would all be put on file now, and social services may become involved after all. At least this way it wouldn't be Danika phoning them behind Kenzie's back, but it amounted to the same thing because it was Danika's fault this was happening anyway.

"*I take it you've spoken to your doctor?*" *Cheryl asked.*

Kenzie rolled her eyes. "*I don't know where I'm supposed to get anti-depressants from if I haven't.*"

"*Would you like me to make you a cup of tea?*" *Cheryl stood.* "*I think we could all do with a break. The family liaison officer will arrive soon, and she may ask you to go through it all again, I'm afraid, just so she's up to date with what's happened. She can stay with you here. She'll be your support system.*"

Danika had yet to announce that she would be going to work later. She had an hour before she had to be there. When Cheryl left the room, Danika raised a finger to her lips to warn her sister not to say anything bad. Cheryl could be listening, she'd maybe left them alone on purpose.

"*Do you need me to stay the night?*" *Danika asked, praying she'd say no.*

"*No. I can't stand you looking at me the way you have been, like I'm a shit mother and it's my fault she's gone missing.*"

"I'm sorry, I didn't know I was looking at you that way. That's not what I was thinking at all."

"Yes it was, you liar."

Danika didn't trust herself to continue the conversation, so she got up and stared out of the window. Despite all the time that had passed since the police had first arrived, there was still a lot of activity out there. Officers spoke to neighbours at their doors, and a policeman with a dog paced up and down, the German Shepherd sniffing at the bushes and grass.

I know what's happened to her. This is all a waste of your time.

McFarlane walked up the garden path and into the house. He entered the living room, and Danika turned to smile at him sadly.

"Any news?" she asked. "I see that dog out there."

"They're not picking up a scent at all, I'm afraid."

Kenzie covered her face with her hands and sobbed. Danika did the dutiful thing and went to sit beside her on the sofa, although the last thing she wanted to do was comfort her. She had too much on her mind, like where Amelia was and who was looking after her. Was Kenzie now in danger? There was no way The Organiser could come down this street to keep tabs at the moment, but she'd bet he wished he could. At least with the police presence he couldn't come anywhere near Kenzie, and with the family liaison officer staying overnight, she should be safe. Danika wouldn't put it past The Organiser to threaten to take Kenzie next.

Cheryl came back in. "Did I hear you say there isn't a scent? That's a bit odd if we're going with the assumption that Amelia left the house by herself."

McFarlane gave her a narrow-eyed stare as if to tell her to be quiet. She blushed and handed a cup to Kenzie and then one to Danika who didn't really want tea, but she took it to be polite. She couldn't wait to get out of here, go to work and lose herself in punters so she didn't have to think about what her lack of action had brought about. And it was so unfair that she was some random choice, chosen to do this.

She walked out and went to the kitchen, hoping McFarlane followed. She needed to find out more about what was going on. Thankfully, he came in and busied himself making a coffee. She supposed they helped themselves often when the resident wasn't in any fit state to play host.

"Do you think someone came and took her?" Danika asked quietly.

"It's looking that way."

"But nobody's broken in, you said that yourself."

"Maybe Amelia opened the door and whoever it was picked her up and carried her. That would account for

the dog not picking anything up." He pushed the kitchen door to. *"I don't want to say anything while your sister is still so upset, but do you know of anyone she hangs around with who could have taken her daughter?"*

Danika was amazed that he thought Kenzie was upset. If it was her child, she'd be screaming and would have to be sedated if she'd gone missing or was snatched. Kenzie sounded belligerent and angry, sulky that her child had walked out and caused so much trouble.

Danika had to at least try and do some damage control so she could tell The Organiser she'd attempted to steer this in the direction he wanted. "Kenzie likes to keep to herself—ask the neighbours, they'll tell you. She doesn't have any friends because she doesn't trust people. You're aware our parents have been spoken to and they're not interested, and I'll tell you why. Our father abused both of us as we were growing up, and neither of us knew the other one was going through anything until we were a lot older. I saw him touching Kenzie. We told our mother, who refused to believe us, and after that, we bided our time until we could start work and get enough money to rent a bedsit. There is no way Kenzie would allow anyone into her home with Amelia here. She's paranoid someone will abuse her. It's perhaps not rational, but it's the way her mind works, so if you're thinking she had a boyfriend who took the child, then it's highly unlikely. I take it my father had an alibi?"

McFarlane looked as if her telling him their backstory was a little too much for him to handle on top of a child going missing. "Yes, he was at the pub."

"Typical."

"What do you think happened?"

"Amelia's started getting curious lately." I'm lying. She's dopey, and I'm wondering if my sister's been drugging her for a long time. *"I would have said she walked out on her own. What if she had her mum's shoes on? She loves dressing up in those."* Another lie. *"Would that account for no scent?"*

McFarlane stirred milk into his coffee. "I'll pass that on. Thank you."

He left the room, talking on his radio, going out the front to stand on the path to drink his coffee. A lady got out of a car and approached him. They chatted for a minute or two, and then she came into the house with him. He took her into the living room, and Danika assumed she was the family liaison officer. Maybe she should take her chance to leave now, although she still had this bloody tea to drink. She took her cup into the living room and sat on the armchair while the family liaison officer introduced herself.

"I'm Ellie Knight, and I'm here to answer any questions you may have or just to be someone for you to talk to. You'll have fears and questions, and I'll be here to help you through everything."

Danika drank her tea, observing Kenzie to gauge what the officers saw when they looked at her. No tears. No shakes. She didn't have such a sulky face now. Maybe she was pleased she'd get as much attention as she wanted and needed from Ellie. Maybe she craved company despite hiding herself away from the world for the most part.

Another half an hour had gone by before Danika announced she was going to work.

"At this time of night?" Cheryl asked.

"Yes, at this time of night," Danika said, unprepared to go into details of what she did to earn money.

She kissed Kenzie on the head, gave her a quick hug, and then took her cup to the kitchen. She grabbed her coat from the rack by the side of the front door and left. She had thirty minutes in which to walk to the Orange Lantern. She may have to jog part of the way.

She reached the Lantern with two minutes to spare, popping her head into the office to let Widow know she'd arrived. The television was on a news channel, and Danika's heart sank. Was that Kenzie's street? She looked closer, her stomach churning. No, it was somewhere else.

"Another stabbing," Widow said. "It's getting beyond a joke now."

Danika smiled. "Oh God. I'd best get on."

She turned into Goddess, going up to her room and changing into sexy lingerie. She couldn't think of Amelia and where she was. She couldn't think of Kenzie's story being triple- and quadruple-checked by Cheryl as she related it to Ellie. Kenzie would be under intense scrutiny now. Danika just prayed they didn't go down the abduction route. If they did, the story was going to explode all over the news and The Organiser would blame it on her.

Changed, and with her hair brushed and makeup on, she pressed the button to alert downstairs that she was now ready. She pushed her shoulders back and stuck on a smile, emptying her head of all the horrible things so she could concentrate only on being loved.

Chapter Twenty

It wasn't often that Ichabod got the collywobbles, but ever since his conversation this morning with his girlfriend, Marleigh, he was more conscious of what he was doing, how reckless it was. Going out once tonight had been a risk, but twice could be seen as asking for trouble. He understood that this was a big job and the twins couldn't do it all alone, but sometimes he wished there was someone else on hand with his skills that they could have asked instead. It was becoming a bit of a burden to drop everything at work and go running. Earlier, he'd completely forgotten himself and had enjoyed collecting Thomas, and he'd felt guilty when he'd remembered that in a few short months, he'd have more responsibilities at home and he couldn't gad about getting thrills the way he did.

There used to be a time when George and Greg would call on Moon and his men, Alien and Brickhouse, to jump into the fray, but for months they'd relied on Ichabod more and more—he'd become their go-to man, something he'd dreamed about once upon a time. Funny how things changed. Maybe Moon was too busy on his own Estate these days, or maybe they'd had a falling-out. Had something gone down in Amsterdam that had soured their relationship or had Moon just taken a step back, concentrating on his own shit rather than stretching himself thin by diving into George and Greg's business?

It was time someone else, or a few someones, were trained to match Ichabod's capabilities. Maybe Cameron and Will could go to martial arts classes and become people who could do everything Ichabod could.

He wrenched himself out of his head and into the present. He stood in the kitchen at the safe house, the back of his neck prickling, perhaps a warning that something was going to go wrong, or maybe his instinct was telling him he ought to pack this shit in now, Amelia being his last job. It had been playing on his mind on and off all day, especially when Marleigh had put it into his head that she didn't know what she'd do without him, and if he ever got caught, she'd be devastated. She'd been through the mill with her ex-husband, and he hated the fact that he added to her worries, but she'd known who he was and what he did from the start and had accepted him anyway. But she was right, luck only took you so far. One wrong move and he could find himself behind bars, the twins unable to do anything about it. He couldn't afford to get nicked, not anymore.

His future looked a lot different to what it had yesterday.

Cameron had been pretty quiet but then told him about a man called Matty, babbling as if he needed to get it out quickly and off his chest. Ichabod's hackles rose. He wanted to punch something to take away the nasty taste in his mouth and the urgent need to do some damage. That poor little girl... Would she ever forget what had happened to her, not just with Matty but being kidnapped and kept in that bloody room with only a Barbie for company? She was old enough to remember so much now. Had it happened a year or two ago she'd have been none the wiser later down the line. Sometimes fate was a cruel bastard and sent people down roads nobody should go down. He hoped it would be kinder to her in the future and that the uneasy feeling he had about her was just his imagination running riot.

"I don't think I'm ever going to get over what she told me." Cameron rubbed the back of his neck as if he, too, had prickles there.

What was Ichabod supposed to say? He settled for: "It's a tough one tae deal wid."

Cameron sighed. He looked pained. "She said it as if it wasn't a big deal."

"Maybe tae her it isn't. Maybe Matty made it all seem normal and okay. Ye know what these perverts are like. They're sneaky. Did she say what he did tae her?"

Ichabod wished he hadn't asked that. What if Cameron launched into it and put images in his head he didn't want to see?

Cameron shook his head and sank onto a chair at the table. "No, thank God, and I didn't want to ask her. I'd be a bastard to expect her to relive it."

"Did ye let the twins know? Sorry, stupid question."

"No, it's not, you're just doing your job, but yeah, I did."

"Then there's not much else ye can do."

"I keep thinking if it was Rosie. I know she's only little, but…"

Ichabod understood, and to break the tension, he chuckled and said, "Wid a mammy like Janine, there's no way your daughter will be put in harm's way. And then there's ye. Ye'd rip the face off anyone who touched her. Rosie's safe and always will be. Wid the twins as uncles, she won't be able tae breathe without them knowin' about it."

Cameron smiled, nodded, and got up, walking out. He likely needed to be alone to process things. Maybe he'd talk to Janine later and she'd help ease the horrors in his mind. Then again, she was so blunt, she might not and could make it worse.

Will came in and jerked his head for Ichabod to follow him. They went upstairs and stood beside the single bed, light from the landing pasting a skewed rectangle on the covers. Amelia lay under them, fast asleep, a Barbie clutched in her small hand. She looked so innocent, and Ichabod's mind went down a road *he* didn't want it to go down. How far had Matty gone? How had Amelia's mother not noticed her child may have been sore? He could only hope she hadn't been violated in the worst way, although any touches in that regard were wrong.

Feck, don't think about that.

Will peeled the quilt back, and Ichabod wrapped a blanket around her. He lifted her and carried her out to the car, laying her on the back seat. She was still asleep; he hoped she stayed that way, because for her to wake up to find herself with yet another masked stranger wasn't something he wanted to happen. He wasn't sure he'd be able to calm her down and drive at the same time.

As he drove, he stared at the road, having discussed with Cameron and Will the route he'd take. They'd got the location up on Google Street View so he was able to see there was a street behind her house connected to the back gardens in her row by an alley. It looked easy enough for him to nip along there and into her rear garden, unlikely he'd be seen. He'd counted the houses from when he would enter the alley, and hers was five down. He'd double-checked it, asking Cameron to do the same. The last thing he needed was to take her to the wrong fecking house.

He suppose she was exhausted after everything she'd been through in the last few hours. Will said he'd tired her out by playing Snap and Playmobil and she'd fallen asleep after only two pages of him reading her a story. It amazed Ichabod that she'd seemed to settle so well at the safe house, as if she was used to people she didn't know, wearing masks to boot. He found that so odd. Did her mammy let strangers into their house regularly? Or, because Matty came in at night, did she think that was normal?

Cameron said Matty wears a mask, remember.

Ten minutes later, he coasted down the road he needed and parked close to the alley. He'd leave the driver's door unlocked so he had quicker access when the time came to get away.

He checked all the parked cars and then the windows of the homes in case more coppers than the one stationed out the front were around. What the feck he'd do if one of them walked out of the shadows and spoke to him he didn't know. He couldn't tell them he was bringing Amelia home for the twins without getting them in the shit. Satisfied he was safe, he took her out of the back seat and carried her along the alley, mouthing the numbers of the gates as he passed them.

"One, two, three, four, five…"

This next bit could be dangerous if he had to knock on the door and wake her mother up, but he'd already decided to use his lock pick. In order to get away unseen, he'd take matters into his own hands—he'd still have done what the twins wanted, ensuring Kenzie would know her daughter was back, just not the way they wanted it done. He couldn't risk getting caught, so his way was the best way. If they got arsey with him about it, he'd explain his reasoning and hope for the best.

He cradled her with one arm and turned the handle on the gate, praying it was unlocked. If he'd have thought about this better he would have paved the way first and then returned to the car to collect her, but it was too late now. He pushed the gate open, gritting his teeth in anticipation of a creak, but it swung inwards silently. His eyes now adjusted to the darkness, he closed the gate to and scanned the garden. A couple of sun loungers were on the patio, so he put Amelia down and asked God to make sure she stayed asleep.

He bent over at the back door and inserted the lock pick, wincing because he couldn't open it immediately. Around thirty tense seconds later, success, and he twisted the knob handle and opened the door. What if the family liaison officer had come back? What if Danika had got it wrong and the woman *was* staying the night? The house was in darkness, so he took it that even if the copper was there, she'd be asleep. He didn't like taking chances, and if she woke up, he didn't want to just dump Amelia on the floor and run, but if he had to, he would.

He picked her up, ensuring she still clutched her doll, and entered the house, his mouth going dry and his heart thudding too hard, then missing a couple of beats as his anxiety spiked. He nudged the door with his foot so it swung towards the frame but didn't shut, then prowled into the hallway and poked his head into the living room.

No one there.

Cameron had passed on that Kenzie had taken a sedative, so it was unlikely she'd wake up, but all the same, Ichabod crept upstairs and looked in the smaller bedrooms and bathroom—he had to know if the copper was there.

She wasn't.

He found Kenzie in a big bedroom at the front. He placed Amelia on the bed beside her, removed the blanket, and covered her with the quilt, staring down at the tableau. She stirred and snuggled close to her mother, and he imagined her waking in the morning to find she wasn't at the safe house but at home, wondering how she'd got there. The scene of Kenzie setting eyes on her little girl had Ichabod smiling.

He backed out of the room but bumped into something. Feck. He spun quickly, expecting to come face to face with the Old Bill, but he'd just butted up against the banisters. Letting out a slow breath and counting to five, he went downstairs and left by the back door, locking it with the pick. Glad he hadn't had to threaten Kenzie, he exited the garden and walked back to the car, checking the vicinity, his nerves on edge.

He sat in the driver's seat and tossed the blanket to the passenger side, wanting to take a moment to calm his breathing, to recalibrate himself, but staying around here wasn't wise. He started the engine, hating that it was so loud, and peeled away, taking the car four streets away where Dwayne waited behind a tree. Ichabod got out and threw the keys at him, then continued on foot, his head down, the blanket balled under his armpit. He quickened his steps. Two streets on, and he found a parked Ford where he'd been told it would be, the keys under the wheel arch. He got in and drove off, taking the vehicle to Jackpot Palace and parking it behind. Once Dwayne had disposed of the first car, he'd come back to collect this one.

The casino was still open, and he let himself in the back, going straight to his office. He tugged off his beard and wig, his gloves and clothes, and stuffed them in a black bag with the mask. He took a clean suit from a cupboard and dressed, then went out the back again to burn the contents plus the black bag and the blanket in an old oil drum. He watched the flames dancing, going back over his movements of the whole night. No one at the casino would know he'd even left twice, as he'd said he wanted to be alone in his office to go over the accounts. They all knew how shitty he could get if he was disturbed doing that job. He'd also switched off the internal CCTV in the corridor outside the office.

Back inside, he sent a message.

ICHABOD: PACKAGE DELIVERED. ASLEEP IN BED WITH HER MOTHER.

He slid his phone away and entered the casino proper, doing his job, smiling at customers and staff as if he hadn't abducted a man and returned a kidnapped child. He lost himself watching a game of blackjack, marvelling at all these people who had no clue what he'd been up to. As far as he knew, he was safe from any suspected involvement. After all, he'd been in disguise, and why would a casino manager have anything to do with a little girl going missing anyway?

He thought of Marleigh and whether he'd tell her what he'd done tonight. He wanted to, he wished he could share everything with her, but this was the twins' business, and he'd be better off keeping his mouth shut. She understood there were things he couldn't tell her, she'd accepted it, but it still felt wrong to be in a relationship and keep secrets, especially because she'd given him some brilliant news this morning.

She was eight weeks pregnant, and he couldn't be happier, but having dealt with Amelia, it brought it home how precious children were and how quickly they could be taken from you. He worried that one day someone would catch him on a job for the twins and he'd be arrested and put in prison, missing his own child's life. He had the strong urge to walk away now, to cut ties, but he couldn't do it. Maybe if he spoke to the twins and explained how he felt, they'd let him just run the casino instead of asking him to do dangerous, illegal things. Jackpot Palace was one of their covers, a legitimate business, so it wouldn't seem dodgy that he worked there.

It was something he'd think about until he found the right words to explain. He didn't want George and Greg to think he was ungrateful for everything they'd done for him, but how long did you have to be grateful for? Yes, they'd see it as a waste of his skills if he no longer went on surveillance and whatever, but he was going to be a father, and his priorities lay with the child and Marleigh.

He snapped himself out of his daze and smiled at a man coming towards him, a high-roller who regularly spent a fortune at the casino. He lost more than he won but enjoyed the thrill and had enough money that losing didn't affect his bank balance.

"I've just had my biggest win yet," he said. "Sixty grand."

That was all right, he'd lose it again come tomorrow.

Ichabod clapped him on the back. "That's feckin' brilliant, mate."

After all, what else was there to say? He had a job to do, and he was going to do it.

Chapter Twenty-One

Matthew listened to the sounds of those two monsters leaving, the front door slamming. He cursed himself, teeth gritted. How could he have got this so wrong? Why had he believed their story that Danika and Kenzie would be here? He prided himself on being able to spot a liar from a mile off, but that George had fooled him good and proper. If he didn't know better, he'd say the bloke had taken a leaf out of his book or that he'd taught him everything he knew.

He tried to get more comfortable on the hard chair, glaring over at Nina, wishing they'd killed her before they'd left so he didn't have to listen to her snivelling. She wasn't supposed to cry, she wasn't allowed, but it seemed she'd forgotten the rules. To be fair, seeing people killed in front of her must have upset her delicate sensibilities. She always turned away at violence on the telly. All that blood and gore didn't sit well with her.

She sniffed several times, sky-rocketing his nerves.

"What have I told you about crying?" he barked.

She kept her eyes closed, probably unable to stand seeing the dead body in the other corner. The bloke had clearly done something wrong, otherwise he wouldn't have been killed. George had said Matthew would be killed, too, but that didn't make sense because he hadn't done anything wrong. Showing love to your daughters wasn't bad, was it? Or were the twins in the same brigade as his wife, where they thought his kind of love was frowned upon?

Of course, he'd never mentioned what he did to his mates. He wasn't stupid, he knew they'd go straight to the police. He'd read the papers, aware of what people thought of what he did. When Danika and Kenzie had told Nina about what he'd done, he'd had to stop going into their bedrooms at night. He hadn't chosen anyone else to replace them, because all he'd wanted to do was love his daughters and he only had two. He'd had to shag Nina more often, closing his eyes and pretending she was Danika or Kenzie. All those years of sticking it to her had churned his stomach.

But then a bright spot had appeared on a horizon he'd stopped looking at, thinking his future was bleak, so what was the point. He'd spotted Kenzie in town, pushing a little girl in a buggy, and he'd followed her home. She'd been in a world of her own, hadn't been vigilant and looked behind her, hadn't seemed to hear his footsteps, although he'd tried to tread lightly. Or maybe she had heard them but thought nothing of it. To be honest, she looked off her face on something, maybe whatever it was in the prescription bag she'd picked up from the chemist.

He'd been going down her street regularly for a year or two, then when he'd judged the time was right to introduce himself to the kid, he hung around until Kenzie had left her house and followed her again. She didn't go out much, so it was pot luck as to when she'd appear. On that particular day he'd been standing on the corner of her road for three hours. She'd gone into town, getting a bit of shopping in Sainsbury's, piling it into the basket under the buggy. She'd hung her handbag on her shoulder with the body of the bag resting on her small of her back, stupidly leaving the zip undone. When she'd been distracted by the kid, he'd dipped his hand inside, what he was doing concealed by the close crowd around them. She'd paused in talking to the child for a second, and he'd held his breath, thinking she'd felt him ferreting about, but then someone had come by and jostled her, and his fingers had passed over what had felt like keys.

He'd taken them out, turned sharply, and walked in the other direction, going into Timpson and getting copies of every key on the ring—he couldn't be one hundred percent sure which one was for her front door as there were two Yales on there. He remembered thinking she'd soon find out they were gone when she reached her front door, perhaps think she'd lost them, but he'd dropped them beside the long grass in her front garden before she'd got home, shaking his head at the fact she hadn't mown it, that she didn't keep on top of the chores. She never had done. As a teenager she'd left her room untidy, no matter how often he'd told her to clean it. He dreaded to think what the inside of her house was like. Lazy, that's what she was, the same as her mother.

He'd bided his time, and when the kid looked to be about four years old, he'd masked up and gone inside the house for the first time. At three in the morning, he'd prowled the downstairs, using a low-beam torch and pointing it into every room. As he'd suspected, she hadn't grown fond of housework as she'd got older. Piles of laundry everywhere, but at least she was doing that job. Toys on the living room carpet. Washing up in the sink. He'd learned to live in a messy house, despite his efforts of trying to teach Nina that a clean home meant a clean mind. His mate had told him, down the Lock and Key, that if it bothered him that much, he ought to do it himself. He was clearly one of those New Age twats who thought men and women were equal.

He smiled to himself, thinking back on it to how he'd crept up the stairs and watched Kenzie sleeping for a while. She'd breathed heavily, and it was as if fate was on his side, giving him the green light to go to the child. She'd been in the smallest bedroom, lying on her side and whispering to a teddy bear. He'd gone in and closed the door, *shhing* to tell her to be quiet. He'd expected her to scream at the sight of him, to call for her mummy, but in the light of his torch beam she'd just stared then sat up.

He'd moved closer and perched on the bed. "I'm Matty, and I've come to give you cuddles when you can't sleep."

He wasn't a complete bastard, she wasn't ready for what he really wanted to do to her, but he could wait until she was older. He'd settle for holding her tight on his lap.

He gone to see her twice a week, leaving Nina in bed, oblivious to the fact that he'd gone out for two hours as she was still snoring when he got back. It was just like the old days, her sleep aided by the pills he'd put in her cup of tea before bed.

He hadn't admitted what he'd done to their daughters until one night he'd got so angry with her he'd blurted it out. By that time, the little cows had left home, and no matter how much he'd tried to explain that he just wanted to love their children, Nina hadn't understood. She'd said she was going to tell the police, but he'd soon disabused her of that notion. A hand to her throat, squeezing tight, and words in her ear ensured she'd never breathe a word.

And she hadn't given the game away at all until her stupid slip-up in the hallway when the twins had come to the house. She'd said *us*, then jumped a mile when George and Greg had appeared. She'd likely worried they'd realised what she'd meant.

He reminded her of what she'd said. "So is it any wonder they've locked us in this room?"

"I should never have listened to you. I should have gone to the police years ago." She still had her eyes closed, the wimp.

"Ah, but you cared about your own life more than Danika's and Kenzie's. You were even more afraid of dying than getting them justice, as you called it. Justice? For what, their old man giving them cuddles?"

"But it wasn't just cuddles, was it?" Finally, she opened her eyes and stared across at him. "Did you find out where Kenzie lived? Have you been seeing her all this time? Is that little girl yours?"

He laughed. "I used to wear condoms, I'm not fucking stupid, so no, she isn't mine." That was just downright depraved to have accused him of that. "You're sick in the head to even think of it. You say I'm a pervert, but what about you? Only a nonce would come up with that bollocks."

"It's a conclusion any normal person would come to."

She was getting brave talking back at him, maybe because she had nothing left to lose and she knew she was going to die. Or was she going to come clean to the twins and convince them he'd forced her to keep his secret? He wouldn't put it past her. Danika was just as secretive, taking after Nina. Or was that himself, because he'd been damn good at hiding everything. Look at how Nina had no idea he'd been visiting Amelia. Look at how he'd fooled the police into thinking he had no idea she existed when they'd questioned him after her kidnap. Look at all those years Danika and Kenzie had kept their mouths shut. If Danika hadn't got jealous at not being the only best girl, he'd still be loving his daughters now. The pair of them had craved his attention, wanting to be special.

"I'm never going to be able to get to know my granddaughter because of you," Nina said.

"You wouldn't anyway because whoever took her has probably killed her by now."

"Don't be so wicked."

"It's true. If you're thinking of persuading the twins to believe you, I reckon you've got a job on your hands there. George has got it in his head that we're going to die, and I doubt very much you'll be able to change his mind. The rumours say he's a stubborn bastard."

"I wish I'd never laid eyes on you. I should never have married you."

"Well, you did, and what's done is done." He glanced over at the man in the corner. "I wonder how he pissed them off."

"I don't care, I just want to go home."

"What, and bury your head in the sand, pretending none of this happened? You're good at that."

"Because you *told* me to. You threatened me."

"And you didn't have the balls to stand up against me. If you had, I'd have been in prison and you'd probably be on your back in bed for another man."

"You're disgusting."

"Whatever."

He had plans of his own to tell the twins he hadn't done anything, that it was all lies. Without Danika and Kenzie here to refute it, he could convince them, no problem. All his life he'd been able to pull the wool over people's eyes, and tonight would be no different. If they could do him a big favour and kill Nina, he'd be a loyal Cardigan forever, never put a foot wrong, going to work and the Lock and Key, minding his own business.

The only spanner in the works was if his daughters were brought here—was that where the monsters had gone, to collect them? Danika could be so convincing; she was a chip off the old block and could charm the monkeys from the trees.

His shoulders slumped. Yeah, if she came here, he was fucked.

Chapter Twenty-Two

Woken by a noise and staring at a murky silhouette leaning over her bed, Danika opened her mouth to scream, but a gloved hand clamped over it. She blinked at whoever it was, her mind zipping through her options. Going by the size of her unwanted guest, she didn't have many. She wasn't strong enough to fight him off.

"*Shh*, it's me," George said.

She relaxed in relief, but then her nerves spiked, her pulse accelerating, and her stomach rolled over. What if they'd come to take her to the cottage after all? What if they were going to punish her for lying when all she'd done was tell them the truth—eventually? She couldn't even speak to ask him.

"I'm not here to cart you off and kill you," George said, "but I *do* need to cart you off for another reason. We've collected your mum and dad, and I think you ought to confront them. If you don't do it tonight then you'll never get the chance because they'll be six feet under. There are people currently in their house, making it look like they've done a runner." He took his hand away and moved back so she could sit up. "I'll leave you to get dressed."

Danika reached for her phone, bringing the screen to life. There were no messages or missed calls. "Why hasn't Kenzie rung me?"

"Because she likely doesn't even know her daughter's back yet. The person who returned her said they'd put her in bed with her mum. I'm taking it she was asleep."

Another wave of relief swept through her, and tears pricked her eyes. She was glad it was dark so George didn't see any falling, although maybe that would be in her favour if he did. He'd see she had a heart, that she cared for her niece, although he'd probably say she didn't care enough if she let her be stolen.

"So if I'm going with you and Kenzie wakes up and phones the police, then she or they ring me, what the hell do I do if a copper suggests they come and collect me? I won't be here."

"If they suggest that, then you say you'll get a taxi."

She imagined him grinning because it would be theirs that would deliver her to Kenzie's street.

"But then again, we've got the van, so we'll have to drop you around the corner. We'll sort it, don't worry. For now, all that needs to be on your mind is getting your arse up and putting some clothes on."

He left the room, closing the door. She did as she was told, choosing a warm tracksuit. She went into the bathroom to wash her face and brush her teeth, sticking her hair into a messy top bun. Downstairs, she found George in the kitchen.

"Where's Greg?"

George turned from reading the label on a packet of ramen noodles that she'd left on the side earlier. "I prefer Pot Noodles myself. Greg's next door with your mate."

"What for?"

"Convincing her that she's your alibi for when your parents left their house. Someone might have seen them getting into the back of a little white van, if you know what I mean. We don't want the coppers thinking you were the one driving it, do we."

"What time was that?"

"Fuck knows, it's been a bit of a busy night and I wasn't exactly looking at the time. The story is you slept round Oaklynn's all night—you fell asleep on her sofa after watching a film and she didn't want to disturb you."

"I didn't want to drag her into this. I only told her about Joseph and Farah, nothing else."

"Greg can be very persuasive in making sure she'll do as she's told. Don't look at me like that, he's not going to hurt her. Fucking hell, talk about suspicious."

"Wouldn't you be if you were me?"

"I suppose so. Listen, we may as well have a little chat before he gets back. We're both in agreement that you can't walk away from this unpunished."

Fear punctured her chest, and a hand automatically went up to her mouth. She sank to a dining chair and stared at the tabletop. "What… What are you going to do to me? And why do I need to be punished when I was forced into doing all of it?"

"Because it went too far. A little girl got kidnapped, and we can't let that slide. Normally I'd give you a Cheshire grin, but I appreciate what an asset you are to the Lantern, and no bastard's going to want to shag a scar-faced woman if he can help it, so I'll cut you elsewhere."

She shuddered at the thought. "Where?"

"I don't know yet. Come on, we'd best be off."

How could he be so blasé after delivering news like that? Didn't he have a conscience? She got up and put her trainers on in the hallway, Greg coming through the front door just as she tied her laces.

"Sorted," he said to George who turned off the kitchen light and stood waiting for Danika, looking like he didn't have much patience left.

"What did she say?" he asked.

"There wasn't much she *could* say, but she now understands that the shit going on in Danika's life is much worse than what she previously knew, but I didn't tell her the ins and outs. She knows to keep her mouth shut and provide an alibi. She's a grand richer for it."

Danika didn't blame her for taking the money, she'd have done the same. Danika would also have provided an alibi if she'd been confronted by Greg. The consequences of not doing that didn't bear thinking about. She stood and left the house, paranoid that a copper sat in a car. She headed towards a white van, assuming it was theirs, but George called her back.

"Oi, you need a blindfold on," he whispered. "We can't have you knowing where we're taking you."

Cold fear sluiced through her, but at least if she wasn't allowed to see the destination it meant they'd be letting her go home again. A part of her had worried they were lying, coercing her to go with them and then revealing their true intentions afterwards. But even if she thought that, she'd still have to go with them. Running was pointless because they'd either catch up with her or, if she got away, they'd find her in the end. She was convinced they could find a needle in a haystack if they put their minds to it.

She returned to the hallway, Greg closing the door to, and George produced a an eye mask. He handed it over, and she put it on. One of them held her wrist, then the other, and drew them behind her back.

"Got to make sure you can't take the mask off," George said.

She nodded and allowed them to guide her outside. She imagined Oaklynn watching from a window, panicking at seeing Danika bound with her eyes covered. Hopefully Greg had explained things to her.

Instead of expecting her to climb into the van herself, one of them picked her up and put her inside. She sat on what felt like a wheel arch. Doors shut quietly, then the van jostled as they must have got in the front. Once the van got going, she'd likely tip sideways, so she dug her feet into the floor and hoped for the best. The engine rumbled, and they were off.

Not having a conversation on the journey worried her. It felt ominous. She had so many questions, especially about Amelia, but she thought it best to keep them to herself now George had revealed his displeasure at her letting her niece be kidnapped. She was a subject best avoided.

She imagined the turns as they drove but soon lost her sense of direction. The engine died, the sound of a handbrake being pulled up loud in the quiet; it creaked, so maybe the van was old. It was then she thought of her parents sitting in the back of it. Had they been scared? She hoped so.

One of them helped her out and guided her over what she thought was grass, then maybe a path. George told her to step up. The air changed, as if she'd gone inside, and a door clicked. A snip, and her wrists were released. The blindfold came off, and she stood in a hallway, a living room opposite. She turned forty-five degrees and faced a steel door, a handle and keyhole halfway down. She frowned at it. What was behind there?

It looked like she was going to find out. Greg inserted a key but didn't push the door open.

"Before we go in," he said, "I'll explain what's what so you don't get such a shock. When you go through the doorway, there will be a dead man to your left in the far corner, but you won't see him at first because the door will be in the way. He's got a sword sticking out of his mouth, and there's quite a bit of blood."

A sword? She shuddered. "Who is it?"

"Purple, otherwise known as Simon Hughes, the father of Thomas Hughes, who is The Organiser. Or was. You might catch a glimpse of him through a hole in the floor if you look hard enough. In the top-left corner is your mother. She has her hands and wrists tied, and she had a little accident when she first came here, so it might smell a bit pissy if you go near her. And then opposite you will be your father. He was sitting on a chair when we left him, but he could have got up and hopped over to your mum, who knows? It'll stink of blood, you'll see blood, and you'll likely wish you'd never walked inside. So if you're having second thoughts, now's the time to go and sit in the living room while we get on. I'll have to tie your wrists and ankles, though, in case you try and leave."

She took a deep breath and asked herself what she wanted. Could she watch her parents be killed? She'd imagined it many times, but actually seeing it might ruin her more than she was already.

"I'll go in."

Greg smiled. "Let me just check neither of them have picked up any of the weapons off the table first." He disappeared inside, then held the door open.

Her first sight was of her dad who turned his head to look at her. She hid a shiver.

"You'd better pack this in, Danika," he said. "Look at what lying does. Look at the shit you've got us all in."

Hatred for him welled up. "How about no." She wanted to go in but couldn't get her feet to move. "How about you admit what you did?"

"I didn't do anything except love you."

"But your brand of love is illegal."

He flinched, and finally her feet went one in front of the other. She stood with her back against the wall beside her father, staring at what was now the top-right corner at her mother. She looked as if she'd been crying. Dad had probably been shouting at her, telling her what she should do and say, threatening her.

"I swear I didn't know for sure until he told me," Mum said. "It was after you'd left and he let it slip."

"What I'm against is the fact you didn't believe us when *we* told you," Danika said. "You said we were making it up and trying to cause trouble. You didn't once try to find out whether we were telling the truth. You sent us to our rooms and told us never to talk about it again, that we were wicked girls." She turned her glare on her father. "And then you came back from the pub and said if we went to the police you'd kill us. We were young and scared, and neither of you gave a shit. The pair of you are sick."

"Please," Mum said, drawing Danika's attention her way. "When he told me, I said I was going to phone the police, but he threatened to kill me."

"So all you cared about in that moment was yourself," Danika said.

"I've not long told her that," Dad muttered.

Danika ignored him.

George came in and shut the door. He eyed Dad. "Why don't you enlighten your wife and daughter about Amelia?"

Panic tightened Danika's chest. "What about her?" She dreaded what she was about to hear.

Dad shook his head. "I've got no idea what you're on about."

George went to the top of the room and stood between Mum and the dead man Danika had yet to set eyes on. She didn't want to look at him yet, nor at the sword and the blood.

"Let's start with the name Matty," George said. "That's what Amelia knows you as, isn't it? Now we haven't got all the facts, we're only going by what that little girl said, but you've been visiting her bedroom, haven't you?"

Shock powered through Danika, sending her knees weak. "What?" She stared from George to her father, then back to George. "*What?*"

George folded his arms. "The question is, did he have a key? Did Kenzie give it to him? Was she aware he went into her house in the middle of the night, or did he somehow gain entry another way and your sister didn't have a clue? I'm hoping it's the latter because otherwise she'll be hanging from those chains at some point when all the dust has settled and the police aren't anywhere near her."

Danika thought about how Kenzie had mentioned keeping Amelia docile—had she done that on the nights she knew Dad was coming round? Were the times Danika nipped in when Amelia sat on the living room rug, quiet and withdrawn, the result of the aftermath of one of his 'love sessions'? Could she believe Kenzie had willingly allowed her daughter to be abused, knowing what it felt like and the damage it caused? Was that why she was on anti-depressants, because she couldn't cope with the guilt of what she was doing? Had Amelia being kidnapped not only given her a kick up the arse to look after her daughter properly but to get herself off the medication so she could protect her better? What was it she'd said? That it had to 'stop' and *"I let what Dad did to us ruin her life, too. I'm allowing him to control what I do even now."* And what about when Danika had mentioned the twins killing their parents? Kenzie had said she wasn't sure it was what she wanted. Why not? Because she *wanted* Dad to keep coming round?

It couldn't be that, could it?

She stared at her father. "Is it true?"

"Yes," Mum shouted. "There were mornings I woke up really groggy, like when you were little, and it made me realise. After you'd told me what he did, I didn't wake up like that anymore, then when it started again, I knew he must be up to something. I twigged he'd been drugging me. It was in the tea. So one night I didn't drink it and I followed him."

Dad glowered at her, and it was clear he hadn't known about this.

"He went to a house. I didn't know it was Kenzie's, I swear to God. I didn't stay long enough to find out and I didn't ever go there again to see who lived there. But when the police came to ask us where we were when Amelia was abducted, they mentioned the address, and I knew."

"And you kept it quiet again," Danika said. "What the fuck is *wrong* with you?"

"I got it messed up. I thought Amelia was his. I thought he'd been carrying on with Kenzie all these years."

Danika took a moment to think about that. Kenzie had said she didn't know who the father was, but what if she was lying? That thought was too gross to think about, so Danika shoved it away, but wasn't it best to face it all now, get it all over and done with tonight?

She wished Kenzie was here so she could see her face and any lies reflected there. But that couldn't happen, she could wake up any minute and find Amelia beside her, and then her house would be crawling with the police. It reminded Danika that they should get this over and done with so she could go home. Or maybe she'd be better going to Oaklynn's so she could genuinely say she'd been there. When her mum and dad went missing, she needed the alibi, and anyway, the least she could do was apologise to Oaklynn. Whether that apology would be accepted was anyone's guess. The poor woman had lost her husband and had enough to deal with without having Danika's shit poured on top of her. Yes, Oaklynn had told Danika she could discuss her problems because it meant she got a reprieve from her own, but this crap was one problem too many.

She pointed at her mother. "You! You ought to be ashamed of yourself. For all you knew, when the police came round about Amelia, it could have been Dad who'd taken her, yet you were still prepared to protect him. I've accepted you did that to me when I was a child, but I won't accept it with her. And as for you…" She turned to glare at her dad. "If you've been going to visit Amelia then you're even viler than I thought. Not only did you damage her mother, but you wanted to get to her child, too. And if Kenzie knows… Much as I'd hate her for it, I'd understand. The way you got into our heads, it would be no surprise if she let you wriggle your way back into her life."

The thing she wouldn't admit out loud was that she'd be devastated because Kenzie hadn't told her. She hadn't trusted her with it. But then Danika hadn't trusted Kenzie with this shit regarding The Organiser, Purple, Farah and Joseph, none of it. They were both guilty of keeping secrets, the biggest one Danika keeping the abduction quiet.

She stared at the sword sticking out of Purple's throat, then moved her gaze to the mark on his cheek. That must have been what The Organiser meant, that when she saw him she'd understand the name. She didn't care anymore. None of it mattered.

She caught George's eye. "I'm not going to stay in here while you kill them, but what I need you to get out of my father is whether Kenzie knew he was going into her house. If she did, then I'll tell the police, because Amelia shouldn't stay there with a mother who's just as bad as mine."

She walked out and into the living room, sensing someone right behind her. Greg had followed and, as promised, tied her wrists and ankles. He put the television on for her then disappeared to come back with three cans of Coke, open with straws poking out. He placed them on a table close to her so she could reach.

"We might be a while, hence the three drinks." He smiled sadly. "I've been having a rethink. I'll let George know you don't need to be sliced. After seeing those two pieces of work in action just now, I think you knowing you're their daughter is punishment enough, don't you?"

He strode out, and the slamming of the steel door shut out any sounds of torture she might otherwise have heard.

Chapter Twenty-Three

The police had said their father had an alibi, but Danika wanted to make sure for herself. She'd woken up at lunchtime to a few text messages from Kenzie, plus a voicemail, her mind groggy from sleep. She'd had a strange, vivid dream that Dad was Purple and he'd sent The Organiser to target her. In the dream, Dad didn't even own a sex worker business in order for him to want new customers, it was just a ruse, something he'd told The Organiser to say so he could control his daughter through someone else. How ridiculous that sounded, but it had wormed its way into her head, so she'd now convinced herself it was a premonition.

She hadn't seen Dad since she was in her late teens, and the thought of seeing him now churned her stomach. The last time she clapped eyes on him he'd had brown hair, and for some reason he'd remained that way inside her head. But of course he was going to look different now. He'd maybe have gone grey and have wrinkles.

She stood in the bus shelter opposite the family home with a Covid mask over her mouth and sunglasses covering her eyes. Dad came out of the house bang on time. Back in the day, he'd finished work at half four, got dropped off by his workmate in a van, then he'd have his dinner. At six, he'd go out to the pub. It seemed his routine hadn't changed. His local, the Lock and Key, was only two streets away so not far for him to stagger home when he was off his nut on booze.

She studied him. The same brown hair, just with a few silver streaks. He didn't have that many wrinkles either, so the monster from her childhood remained very close to her memory of him. She'd once spent a lot of time worrying whether he'd turned to other children after she and Kenzie had left but convinced herself he wouldn't have taken the risk. It was easier to control your daughters than someone else's—unless he'd threatened them in order to keep them quiet.

She shuddered.

He closed the front gate and walked down the pavement. Taking a deep breath, Danika left the bus shelter and crossed the street. She had thick-soled boots on as she didn't want to alert him that she followed, but then would he recognise her with her face covered? She doubted it. He'd only twig it was her once she spoke. Or maybe he'd forgotten her voice. Maybe he'd pushed every aspect of her to the back of his mind.

She waited until he veered down a cut-through that would lead to the street where the Lock and Key stood. She walked faster to catch up with him so their confrontation happened in the privacy of the alley.

"Matthew," she said.

He spun round, his face a picture of shock, then he composed it into his usual impenetrable mask. "What the fuck do you want with me after sending coppers round our house accusing us of taking a kid?"

"I didn't send anyone. The police went there of their own accord."

"We didn't even know she'd had a fucking kid, so how are we supposed to nick her?"

"Do you know anyone called The Organiser?"

He frowned. "You what?"

"Have you been telling someone to get me to do things?"

"You're off your rocker, absolutely mental. I don't know what the fuck's up with you, Danny, but—"

"Don't call me that."

"I can call you what I like, and there's nothing you can do to stop me."

"I could slit your throat, something I should have done years ago before we left home."

He laughed. "Like you've got the bollocks for anything like that. What do you actually fucking want anyway?"

"To see if you've been fucking with my life."

"I couldn't give a toss what you're up to. You're too old for me to be interested in you now."

She so wanted to lunge forward and beat the crap out of him. She was tempted to ask him if he'd picked someone else but couldn't bear to know. She turned her back on him and walked the way she'd come, hating the fact that she believed him. Her dream was just a dream. He wasn't Purple. He wasn't orchestrating things.

She stood under the shelter to wait for the bus, wishing she had work tonight so she could fill her mind with other people's needs. Instead, she made her way towards Kenzie's. She didn't want to go there. She didn't want to hear her sister crying, moaning, and she didn't want to answer any questions again, but if she didn't turn up it would look weird. With her niece missing, she'd have to be completely heartless not to check in on her sister.

She finally read the messages Kenzie had sent.

KENZIE: NEIGHBOUR SAW MAN TAKING AMELIA.

KENZIE: WHERE ARE YOU?

KENZIE: WHY AREN'T YOU ANSWERING ME?

KENZIE: FOR FUCK'S SAKE. CAN YOU STOP SHAGGING MEN FOR FIVE MINUTES AND ANSWER YOUR BLOODY PHONE?

Danika's mind was stuck on the first message. Someone had seen The Organiser. Had he turned up in just the disguise he wore while with her, or had he been sensible and put a balaclava on? Would the police find it weird that she hadn't responded to any of Kenzie's messages yet? Would Kenzie have even told them she hadn't?

Half an hour later, Danika walked down Kenzie's street, a police car parked out the front, but no officers at any doors. Ellie's car was also there. On her way down the pavement, Danika quickly Googled MISSING CHILD, EAST END, and added the date. There was a small article saying a little girl had wandered out of the family home at approximately nine o'clock last night, but otherwise, it had been pretty much contained. Had that not been what The Organiser wanted, Danika would be annoyed about that, a missing child case barely warranting a couple of lines in the news article. It was disgusting. She was aware there were many children who went missing, but Amelia was only four. Surely she deserved more attention than that.

She dropped her phone in her coat pocket and walked up the garden path. She didn't get to knock on the door; Ellie opened it before she had the chance. They smiled at each other, and Danika stepped inside, taking her coat off and hanging it up. She took her phone out and slid it into her jeans pocket. She popped her head around the doorjamb, but Kenzie wasn't in the extremely tidy living room. Oh God, had she got Ellie to help her clean up? How bloody embarrassing.

"She's having a little sleep," Ellie said. "The doctor thought it best. He gave her a tablet so she can get some rest. She's barely slept, which is understandable. Would you like a cup of tea?"

"It's okay, I can make it." Danika got on with that, finding it odd that a stranger sat at the table as if she belonged there. *"Do you want one?"*

"No thanks, I've not long had one. How have you been?"

"I couldn't sleep either. I keep worrying where Amelia is. What she's doing. Whether anyone's taken her. I keep imagining her being hurt. Someone being horrible to her. What's the status now? Kenzie sent me a message to say that a neighbour saw a man with Amelia."

"Yes, he was carrying her while she slept. He put her in the back of a white van. Unfortunately, he drove away before the witness could get the licence number. The van was seen on ANPR cameras, but it's a fake plate. Sadly, the abductor had his face covered so we've been unable to identify who took her."

"So did the neighbour only see him leaving the house or something?"

"Yes, she caught sight of him just as he was opening the garden gate."

"Didn't she phone it in? I'm not being funny, but if a child is being taken from a place where you know damn well it's only ever the mum with her, surely you'd want to phone the police because it would be odd."

"You would have thought so, wouldn't you, but apparently, her son distracted her. He pricked his finger on one of the bushes over the road and he was bleeding so she had to take him in and clean him up. By the time she'd disinfected it and put a plaster on..."

"In that time, the person could have taken Amelia anywhere."

"Unfortunately, yes. The CCTV lost sight of the van when it headed towards the Moon Estate."

Was that a clue? Did The Organiser live there? Was it Moon himself who was Purple? Would The Organiser have driven that way on purpose to create confusion? Amelia could be back on Cardigan or on any of the other Estates by now. Fucking hell, she could even be outside London.

"So what's happening now?" Danika poured boiled water onto coffee granules, taking the cup over to the table and sitting with Ellie. "Does anyone have any theories as to who took her?"

"None whatsoever. With no father and no friends for us to interview, there's only you and your parents, and none of you seem to be involved."

"Could it have been a random selection? Could they have followed Kenzie and Amelia home at some point so they could find out where she lived? Did they bide their time before they took her? I say that because

Kenzie hasn't really left the house lately. Sorry, you've probably thought of all these things. I'm just saying what's been going through my head, that's all."

"It's fine, I understand."

"This is going to sound awful, and it doesn't mean that I've given up hope, but what happens if you can't find her? Do you just forget about her? Does she become a cold case? Why would someone have wanted to take a child apart from a paedophile?"

"It could be she was chosen to be sold off for adoption. There are numerous reasons children are abducted, and sadly, sometimes we never find out why it happened or where they've gone."

"Apart from the times you find a body. Sorry, I'm quite a practical person. I've been thinking about all the scenarios ever since she went missing. It's driving me mad, to be honest."

Ellie smiled. "Some people can handle looking at things objectively and others can't. One of the other reasons Kenzie was sedated was because she's been tormenting herself with thoughts of Amelia being with a paedophile. She's also crippled with guilt because she admitted to giving Amelia an extra spoonful of Calpol to make her sleepy."

"Oh."

Ellie nodded. "So not only is she beating herself up about taking a double dose of her own medication, which meant she hadn't woken up when the person came into the house, she's also trying to cope with the fact that Amelia couldn't call out for help because she was too deeply asleep. She's also admitted that she can't cope with raising a child and she's finding it extremely difficult. So this is where I ask you a question that may offend you, and I apologise in advance if it does. Is there any way that because your sister can't cope she would have arranged for someone to take her daughter?"

"Never. She's very proud but would have told me if she had plans for someone to take her away—she would ask me to take her for a start."

"She didn't want to do that because of your profession."

Danika wasn't about to get defensive. What she did for a living she enjoyed, and she'd chosen to do it, and no one had the right to make her feel shitty because of it. "I would have given that up."

"That's very kind of you."

"She's my niece."

"Why do you think Kenzie kept this to herself? The struggle, I mean."

Once again, Danika told a stranger about their childhood and their father. "I've not long been to speak to him to be honest. I wanted to ask him to his face whether he'd taken Amelia to use her like he used us."

"I'm sorry you went through that. Would you like to press charges?"

"What's the point? It was years ago, and it's our word against his. Then there's our mum, who refused to believe he'd do anything like that. No, I'd like to leave it in the past where it belongs."

"But it's not in the past if it's still living rent-free in your head."

"Please, I really don't want to do anything about it. I'm keeping strong the best way I know how. Have you asked Kenzie the same question?"

"She doesn't want to pursue anything either. She just wants her little girl back. She wants to try to get better, get help for her mental health and be a good mother."

Maybe this was as Danika had thought before, that the abduction had given Kenzie the kick up the arse she needed. In a way, it was a relief to know she wanted to try harder; it meant Danika didn't have to take the child on.

God, I sound such an evil cow.

"How long do you think Kenzie will be asleep?" she asked.

"Probably until the morning now."

"Then there's no point in me staying. I only came here to offer her some support."

"She said your relationship is somewhat strained."

"What has that got to do with anything? She doesn't agree with what I do for a living. I didn't agree that she should give it away for free before she had Amelia. She used to go out to the pub and have sex with anyone who smiled at her. I thought she should at least get paid for it instead of men taking it whenever they wanted, like our dad did. We're both actually pretty fucked up when you think about it. The difference is she wears her depression on her sleeve whereas I hide mine beneath it. We're both coping in the only ways we know how. We don't talk about our father anymore, not like we used to, and it seems to have put a brick wall up between us. I look down my nose at her because she can't get her shit together, at least so people can't see she's broken inside. Maybe I should have been more sympathetic."

"Maybe you had enough on your own plate, trying to cope with the trauma yourself. You can't fix someone else's mind until you've fixed your own. You could both probably benefit from therapy."

She didn't want to do that and open a can of worms.

She finished her coffee then swilled the cup out at the sink and placed it in the dishwasher. Maybe she should phone work and see if there were any spare shifts. She'd go crazy if she went home. She said goodbye and left Ellie at the table and went to collect her coat, slipping it on and then walking out the front. She closed the door behind her and caught sight of someone over the road, watching her. She exited the garden and continued up the pavement, sensing the woman still staring at her.

Danika stopped and asked, "Is there something I can help you with?"

"I just… I wasn't sure whether I should say anything. Give you my best wishes or whatever. I can tell you're Kenzie's sister."

"Thank you."

"I saw her being taken, you know."

"Yes, the police said."

"I can't believe he put her in the back of the van without a blanket or anything, poor little mite. Do you think it was her dad?"

"Her dad doesn't know she exists, so no. We don't know who it could be. Kenzie barely speaks to anyone."

"That's why I told the coppers. She doesn't go out that much and keeps to herself. I've never seen a man

going in there, or any woman apart from you." She blushed. *"God, I sound a right nosy cow, don't I?"*

"It's a good job you are nosy otherwise we'd never have known someone took Amelia. We'd still be thinking she wandered out of the house on her own."

"I feel bad because I didn't stop him. I wanted to ask him what he was up to, but my little boy hurt his finger, and the next thing I know…"

"It can't be helped. Anyway, I'd best be off."

"You didn't stay long."

Fuck me, she *is* nosy. *"No, Kenzie's asleep."*

Danika walked off before she could be waylaid any longer. She took her phone out and rang the Orange Lantern. Yes, there was a slot for a couple of hours if she wanted to take it.

She popped her phone away and changed direction, heading towards the Lantern. While Kenzie slept, Danika would once again lose herself in men and pretend to be Goddess, her defence mechanism.

Chapter Twenty-Four

Something pressed against her side. Kenzie froze, keeping her eyes shut and trying to control her breathing. Had Amelia's kidnapper come for her? Was he lying next to her on the bed? Someone was here; they were warm, close, *there*. She listened for the heavy breathing of a man but couldn't hear anything but her own, ragged, showing how much she was frightened.

If he takes me to where he has Amelia, at least we'll be together.

"Mummy? Are you awake, Mummy?"

She had to be hearing things. This had to be a dream. She opened her eyes, picking her wardrobe out of the darkness opposite the bed, and the two chests of drawers next to it. She kept her head still and swivelled her eyes to take in the rest of the room. Everything looked the same as it always did in the dark.

The warmth by her side was still there.

"Wake up, silly Mummy."

Something hit Kenzie's upper chest, and what felt like hair brushed her jawline. She screamed and jumped out of bed. This had to be a sick joke. What had the kidnapper done, put a tape recorder in here and left Amelia's voice playing on a loop? What had he just touched her with? She stared at the bed and the shape on it. Had he bought one of those creepy, life-sized rubber dolls? Was it mechanical and he could move it remotely?

She didn't feel in control of her body; it was heavy from the sedative. It felt as if she'd lost control of her mind, too, the stupid thing trying to catch up with reality versus her imagination.

The figure on the bed sat up. Kenzie shrieked and backed away to the wall. Was this one of those waking nightmares where she actually walked around?

The lamp on the opposite side of the bed snapped on, and it took her several moments to process that Amelia stood there. She ran around the bed towards her, grabbing her up into a hug and sobbing into her hair. If this was a dream, then it was the best one she'd ever had and she never wanted to wake up.

Danika sat on Kenzie's armchair, trying to keep any proof of guilt off her face. Kenzie had phoned her as soon as she'd hugged Amelia, Danika telling her to call the police. From Oaklynn's she'd rung for a taxi, and now, here she was, acting as if she hadn't known Amelia was home before her sister had told her.

She had so much going on in her head — again — even though everything was now over. She had dead people on her conscience, yet at the same time was glad they were dead. She had all the lies she'd told Kenzie stacked up in a pile, reminding her over and over of what she'd done. She had the news of their parents' deaths, although she wasn't sure the early hours of the morning was the right time to tell her, and especially not with coppers still hanging around.

Amelia would be taken to the hospital soon. It hadn't been an immediate thing because not only was it obvious she hadn't been mistreated, but Ellie and other officers felt it was prudent that she stay with her mother for a bit, considering what she'd been through—mental health over physical at the minute. She'd said the men she was with had been kind to her, giving her a Barbie, playing Snap and Playmobil, and reading her a bedtime story. Danika had been told the Barbie had come from The Organiser and the rest was Will, but she couldn't correct Amelia. It was just another thing she had to keep to herself.

Ellie wasn't happy about the term 'men' and was now trying to gently coax Amelia into telling her more.

She clutched her Barbie close. "She had dresses and shoes and bags, but they got left behind. It's okay, though, because the postman is going to bring me some more."

Ellie whispered to Kenzie, "If any parcels come, don't open them, and let us know immediately."

Kenzie nodded. Danika couldn't believe how lively Amelia was—just how much had Kenzie drugged her prior to all this? She was a different kid.

Kenzie cleared her throat. "You said the men didn't hurt you, love. Did you hear anything they said when they were talking to each other?"

"Nah. I told one of them about Matty, though."

Danika stiffened but reminded herself to maintain a casual stance. This was where it could all go wrong. This was where the police could go round to Mum and Dad's and discover they were gone.

Kenzie frowned, glanced at Ellie, then at Danika. "Shit, it couldn't be, could it?"

Danika bit her lip. "I don't know. Oh God, I don't know."

"What's going on?" Ellie asked.

Kenzie flapped her hand at her. "Just let me talk to her for a minute." She stroked Amelia's hair. "Who's Matty?"

"He's the man in the mask who comes in at night to cuddle me when I can't sleep."

"In this house?"

"Yeah. I sit on his lap, and he hugs me. He goes before the sun comes."

"Auntie Danika bought you sweets and juice. Would you like to have some in the kitchen with the nice policeman so Mummy can talk to Ellie?"

"The men gave me juice, but I didn't have any sweets. I had a cookie, though."

Kenzie looked at Ellie. "I'll be back in a minute."

She took Amelia out of the room. Danika kept her attention away from Ellie. She didn't want to meet her eyes and didn't want to tell her what Kenzie suspected. She couldn't afford for her prior knowledge of it to show in her features. She kept her head down and fiddled with her fingers in her lap.

"Are you all right? Ellie asked.

"It's just… It sounds like something horrible has been happening."

Kenzie came back and closed the door. "I didn't want to leave her with McFarlane, but she seemed to like him earlier, and I don't want to say what I've got to say in front of her. Um…oh,

Jesus, I can't get my head straight. That bloody sedative…"

"Take your time," Ellie said, "but then again, if you know who Matty is and he isn't a good person, I need to know now."

"The only Matthew I know is our father," Kenzie said. "And when I looked at Danika, I know she feels the same. It's got to be him. He told us he'd cuddle us in the dark if we couldn't sleep, and it was always on his lap. What if he…what if he's been coming here while I've been asleep? What if he's been touching her?" She entwined her fingers together, twisting them around and around. "I think I'm going to be sick. What if he took her? What if the men are part of a paedophile ring? I said that, didn't I, Danika? I said I couldn't stop thinking about perverts." She burst out crying, trembling uncontrollably.

"Can you sit with her for a minute, Danika? I'll be back in a second."

Ellie left, and Danika got up to move over to the sofa. She put her arm around her sister's shoulders, contemplating whether to tell her about their parents now or whether she should keep it a secret forever. But forever meant Kenzie would always worry Dad would come back for Amelia.

"How's he been getting in?" Kenzie said. "There's been no sign of anyone breaking in or anything." She cuffed snot with her dressing gown sleeve and stared at the closed door, her eyes widening. "Oh shit, I lost my keys once. A couple of years ago. I went to town and when I got back I couldn't get in. I looked by the grass in the front garden and I must have dropped them on my way out." She turned to Danika, fear in her eyes. "What if he's been watching us and we didn't know? What if he saw me drop them and got copies?"

It sounded a bit far-fetched, but it was the most obvious solution. How else could he have got in if he didn't have a key and no one opened the door to him? He *must* have had copies made. Or he had a pick. What a devious fucking bastard. She imagined him swinging from the chains in that steel room, his blood gushing, his eyes pecked out by the tip of the sword, his dick cut off and stuffed in his mouth. On the way to dropping her at Oaklynn's, George had given her a graphic explanation of what he'd done, but with Mum, he'd just slit her throat.

What if Kenzie's lying? What if she's made up the story about the keys? "Do you swear to me you didn't know anything about this?"

Kenzie stared at her in shock. "Are you fucking kidding me?"

"Okay, okay. I'm sorry, but I had to ask. You were always more easily led when it came to him. I thought…I just thought he might have convinced you to let him inside." She lowered her voice. "The docile thing…"

"You thought I drugged my own child so Dad could *abuse* her?" Kenzie whispered. "Do you even *know* me?"

Well, you don't know me, so… "I mean it, I'm sorry. This shit has got me so fucked up I'm not thinking straight. Do you think Mum knew?"

"Of course she did. I know I said I wasn't sure if I wanted them dead, but I am now."

"They've gone," Danika blurted.

Kenzie's cheeks flushed bright red. "What?"

"It's okay, the police will probably think they've legged it after dropping Amelia home. It makes sense, doesn't it? If he had a key to get in to visit her, he'd have had a key to take her and then bring her back. If we push that narrative—"

Danika shut up pretty quickly as the door opened.

Ellie came in and sat on the armchair. "Officers have been sent to your parents' house. Amelia has just come out to McFarlane with the gem that Matty has a 'stupid wife' called Nina. I think it's pretty obvious what's been going on."

"Christ," Danika said.

Kenzie shook, probably from digesting the news Danika had just dumped on her lap. "Those fucking pair of cunts... I mean it, they need to be arrested. I'll do one of those old case things, I don't know what they're called, where you come forward and admit to being abused years later. I'll tell you everything he ever did to me."

"So will I," Danika said. "He needs to be in prison. And *she* needs to be held accountable for her part in it, too." She shook her head, making out she was trying to process what was going on.

"What age did he start with you two?" Ellie asked.

"The night-time cuddles were from as far back as I can remember," Danika said, "but the proper abuse was on my ninth birthday. He... He made me put it in my mouth."

"God, I'm so sorry." Ellie looked at Kenzie. "And you?"

"The same, so maybe he hasn't touched her like that yet. Maybe it was just cuddles and she won't have all this shit in her head like we've got." Tears fell down her cheeks and dripped off her chin. She cuffed snot again. "How the hell can I go from being so happy one minute and devastated the next? I need to go and see her."

Ellie nodded. "She honestly doesn't appear traumatised by any of this, not by your father or the men, which is worrying as it might come out to hit her full force later down the line."

Kenzie walked out, crying.

Ellie sighed. "This is an absolutely horrendous thing for all of you. It must be bringing back terrible memories."

"If it was only cuddles so far, I can cope with that, but what I'm struggling with is him creeping in here when my sister was asleep. She said she lost her keys a couple of years ago and when she got home, she found them by the grass out the front. What if he found them?"

"I'll pass that on. It'll be something that needs to be checked." Ellie pinched her chin. "The officers I spoke to who went round there to ask about the abduction, they were saying your mum and dad were such a nice couple, that they didn't think they'd had anything to do with it, so this has come as a big shock."

"He's good at lying, and so is she." *So am I.*

Ellie's phone rang, and she excused herself to go and answer it. Danika got up and busied herself tidying. She had to have something to do, something to focus on. But then Ellie came back and asked her to sit down. She then went and fetched Kenzie and closed the living room door. She sat on the armchair, Danika and Kenzie on the sofa.

"They're not at home," Ellie said. "There are clear signs they've left the property. All of their clothes are gone."

The twins…

Ellie continued. "A small suitcase was left on the bed. Your father's car's still parked outside, though, so they've obviously decided to use another mode of transport—they know we'll be able to track their number plate. Is there anywhere you know of where they'd have gone?"

Danika shook her head. "When we lived with them, we had no other family. Mum didn't have any friends, but Dad did. You might have to go and speak to the men at the Lock and Key."

Kenzie gripped her knees, her knuckles standing out beneath the skin. "I don't know of anyone either, or anywhere, but he's obviously fucked up somehow and had to bring Amelia back. Oh God, had they planned to take her with them but something happened to stop them from doing it? Was that suitcase on the bed meant for her?"

Ellie inhaled then let it out. "I was just about to say I have some photos of the inside of the suitcase. There are little girl's clothes—"

Kenzie let out a strangled wail. "Oh my *God*..."

Ellie seemed as though she didn't want to be dealing with this. She was struggling, that much was obvious. "If you could just have a look and see whether any of the clothing belongs to Amelia. If we can get proof that he took them from your home without your knowledge, that would help our case a lot."

She held a phone out with a picture on it.

Danika gasped. "They're ours, from when we were little. They're *our* bloody clothes. Kenzie, there's your Mr Tickle T-shirt."

Kenzie peered closer. "Why did they keep them?"

"Normal parents might as keepsakes," Ellie said, "but considering what you told me about your father…"

Danika closed her eyes, imagining him sniffing the material or rubbing it on himself. "I can't…" She got up and rushed into the kitchen, a wave of emotion carrying her along. She swept Amelia up from her chair at the table and held her tight. "I love you, okay? And I'll never let anybody hurt you."

And then she knew.

If anything happened to Kenzie, she *would* take this little girl home.

Chapter Twenty-Five

Since Greg had told Danika she wouldn't be getting cut or punished, she hadn't minded accepting their invitation to meet them at the Taj for dinner. A week had passed since everything that happened, the days going by in a weird blur. Kenzie was getting help with learning how to be a proper mother by going to 'nurturing' classes with Amelia, which started next week. They'd bake cakes together and things like that. Bonding. She'd stopped drugging her, and despite Ellie reprimanding her about doubling the Calpol dose (thank fuck she only thought it was Calpol), plus throwing out vague hints that a possible visit from social services was in order, Kenzie had pointed out that her doctor had said she could double up if she needed to, so she hadn't done anything illegal.

Only Kenzie and Danika knew she'd had amitriptyline, but that was behind them now. The little girl had come on in leaps and bounds, so chatty and animated whenever she was engaged in conversation, but other times, she was still happy to play with her toys quietly. Maybe she was an extroverted introvert. Her psychologist, Madeline, was in the process of determining whether Dad had done anything beyond the cuddling stage. If he had, it seemed Amelia wasn't prepared to talk about it. So far, her sessions had been centred around the 'nice' men in masks—the police were more convinced than ever that Dad had roped friends in to help him abduct her. She hadn't asked where Matty was, why he didn't visit her anymore, so maybe she just accepted he was no longer going to pop round in the middle of the night.

Or maybe, because she didn't have medication fucking up her system, she no longer woke up so assumed he hadn't come because of that.

Danika looked around. They'd met up in the back room of the Indian restaurant, a private space so they could talk freely. They'd eaten their starters; even Amelia had tried some shish kabob, although she now sipped on a glass of milk, saying her mouth was spicy. She'd bought Barbie along with her. The postman hadn't delivered the parcel of doll belongings as Ellie had insisted Kenzie tell her if anything arrived, so Danika had brought the presents round herself. Cameron had handed them over to her. To cover for 'buying' them, she'd told Kenzie she didn't believe, despite the kidnapper's promise, that he would even bother sending anything. This way, Amelia got her things and it made Cameron feel better.

As for who the kidnapper was... The police were still no further forward in discovering it had been Thomas. They were too intent on blaming Mum and Dad, especially as one of his mates had a white van which currently had forensic officers all over it. Danika didn't care about any of it; they were all dead, and none of them could hurt anybody anymore, but Kenzie had been on edge, creeped out about staying in a house their father had broken into. So much so she'd taken the twins' offer and accepted one of their large ground-floor flats which had a garden so Amelia could play outside. They'd bought her a swing set and put it up as a surprise on the day they'd moved in.

"So I've got a proposition for you," George said to Kenzie. "First, this belongs to you." He pushed an envelope across the table to her. "Compensation for what you've been through. Second, we'd like to offer you a job, but seeing as you turn your nose up at what your sister does for a living, I doubt very much you'll accept it. Still, the offer's there, and we could really do with someone like you working during the day once Amelia goes to school."

"I won't sell my body," Kenzie said quietly so her daughter couldn't hear.

"This job would just entail greeting customers and ensuring they have drinks and they're comfortable while they wait. Think of it as being a waitress. The bird who used to do the job, Precious, has fucked off, and while one of the other women has jumped into her spot and taken over admirably with the flirting, she's not a fan of greeting."

"I don't know, it's still in a brothel, isn't it?"

Danika rolled her eyes. "Oh dear, it would mean being near dirty women… Grow up. Honestly, you're being offered a lot of money here to do sod all. It'll get you off benefits."

Kenzie shook her head. "No. It might suit you, but it doesn't suit me. I'd rather take my chances down Sainsbury's."

George shrugged. "Fair enough, we'll find someone else to fill that spot. What sort of thing do you even want to do?"

It looked like Kenzie had never thought about it. She'd never dreamed or hoped or wished. "I've got no idea. I used to be a barmaid before I had Amelia. Maybe I'll go back to that."

"Then we'll give you a job at the Noodle." George smiled. "Now, will you put that envelope away so it doesn't get lost."

She picked it up and peered inside, then slowly raised her head to stare across the table at him, her eyes watering. "That looks like…a lot of money."

"It's a fair bit, yeah, but you've been through the mill, so…" He took another envelope out from the inside of his suit jacket. "I heard someone's starting school soon and she'll need some new clothes." He dropped the envelope beside her plate.

"Oh, you don't need to do that. Danika's already paid for everything."

"Then buy Amelia something else. Now then, with that out of the way, is there anything anyone wants to discuss? It's been a week, so have you had any feelings of guilt cropping up and you've got designs on confessing to the pigs? Do you need us to remind you to keep your gobs shut?"

"What, about our parents?" Danika doubted very much he'd bring her secrets up in front of Kenzie, but she'd said that to make it clear their mum and dad were the only people she was prepared to discuss.

"Yeah, do either of you feel any remorse for what happened to them?" He glanced at Amelia to warn them they needed to watch what they said.

Like they didn't know that.

"No." Danika took a sip of her lager.

Kenzie finally stuffed the envelopes in her big handbag. "No. Why should I feel guilty about them when they didn't about me and my sister? And my child. They can rot in Hell for all I care."

George stared at Danika. "Is there anything else that needs clearing up by any chance? Any secrets that need to be revealed?"

She stared back at him. "No, that's everything now. Thank you."

A knock came at the door, and George called out for whoever it was to enter. A waiter came in with a trolley, collecting their empty plates, while another passed out their main courses. Amelia was going to try a mild chicken korma. Her eyes grew wide at the size of her dinner. Tears pricked Danika's eyes. Kenzie had been so good these past few days, cooking proper meals. Although she was on the same dose of tablets, she had stopped taking the sedatives, and next week she was visiting the doctor to discuss lowering the dosage.

Everyone tucked in, Danika casting a quick glance at Greg, who'd been quiet the whole time. Maybe he had other things on his mind, lady troubles or something? Still, it wasn't awkward with him remaining silent. George filled the void, chatting to Amelia about her upcoming birthday and whether or not she'd like a party where she could invite her new school friends.

"I happen to know someone who runs the community centre," he said to Kenzie. "We can have a right old knees-up there."

Amelia squealed and bounced in her seat. The normal, childlike behaviour brought it home just how much Kenzie had been sharing her pills. Danika would never forgive her and still got angry about it. On what planet had she thought it was okay to do that, just to keep Amelia quiet and less hassle? Kenzie had cried about it the other night, saying she felt so guilty, that she'd make it up to her and she was glad she was only little so she'd never remember. Danika worried about long-term health effects but hadn't bought them up. Kenzie felt bad enough as it was, and so she should. But mother and daughter were like night and day now compared to how they were before the kidnap. Kenzie even kept the flat nice and tidy, so perhaps it really was a fresh, clean start in all respects.

The dinner drew to a close, and they parted ways, Danika, Kenzie, and Amelia walking towards the bus stop in town. While Kenzie and

Amelia chatted to each other, Danika entertained the unanswered questions. Someone, somewhere, was eventually going to notice that Simon and Thomas Hughes were no longer around. Surely they must have done that already, Simon had run a lot of women, but they hadn't been reported missing to the police, according to George, who said their copper had been keeping an ear out for any information.

Regarding Farah and Joseph, the office in the big glass building would soon be cleared out as their lease was up. Apparently their things were going into storage, and again George had gleaned information regarding them, too. Rumours went around that they'd skipped London because of owing lots of money.

As for Mum and Dad, with the rent not being paid to the council, an eviction notice would soon drop on the mat in a few weeks, not that they'd be there to read it. Eventually, someone would call around and discover they weren't there, neighbours saying they must have done a moonlight flit because they hadn't been around for ages. Eventually, the house would be taken over by another tenant, the contents maybe offered to Danika and Kenzie. Neither of them would want it, nor did they want the responsibility of having to get rid of it. If anyone got in contact, Danika would be telling them they'd been estranged from their parents for years so piss off.

But whatever the authorities thought about any of those dead people, it was none of her concern now. She had a future to look forward to, one where she could redefine how she looked at her life and her role in it. Maybe now, instead of linking her profession to what her father had done and how he'd warped her thinking, she should stop telling herself she was doing it to feel loved and say she was doing it to earn a living. To be proud and admit she enjoyed what she did, and she was no longer ashamed.

Kenzie still had a way to go before she'd accept Danika's career choice, but that was a *her* problem, something she'd have to sort out, or not, while on her own journey. They both had new paths to take, and each of them needed to concentrate on themselves. It didn't mean they wouldn't see each other, because they would, but they'd agreed they had a lot of soul searching and work to do, and it was best done without recriminations or judgement from each other.

The bus came, and Danika saw Kenzie and Amelia onto it, waving at them through the window as it drove off. She turned and entered the Red Lion, sitting at the bar and ordering a drink, relieved that at last she could sit down in peace without thinking someone was watching her. George had told her what Thomas had confessed, and while she should feel sorry for him, she just couldn't bring herself to show any empathy. He'd been wicked to her. He'd made her think Purple was a danger, when all along it'd just been some stupid game.

She sipped her gin and tonic, thinking about what she was going to spend her twenty grand on now it wasn't needed for a ransom. She'd take it out of Widow's safe after work tonight and get a taxi home. Maybe she'd give half to Oaklynn, not to pay for her continued silence but as a show of appreciation for how much of a good friend she'd been ever since Greg had gone round there to insist she gave Danika an alibi. There had been no probing questions, just the hope that Danika was okay or she soon would be.

Launderette Lil stepped up onto a little stage in the corner, and the opening bars of 'Hi Ho Silver Lining' struck up.

Danika smiled. Yes, her sun was definitely shining now.

Chapter Twenty-Six

The December gale kicked up, howling around the Orange Lantern and through the trees. The weather had been a right bastard the past two weeks, utterly freezing with the biting wind that was savage enough to take the top layer of skin off your face. It was a good job Widow barely went outside now then, wasn't it.

She stared out from the kitchen at the back, the pines swaying and shushing, the big old oak creaking. All the women and the bodyguard had gone home; they wouldn't be back for a couple of days now, as the twins had some renovations in mind.

Things had changed a lot around here. George and Greg had sent builders in to sort the loft space so she could live on the property instead of having to traipse to her old place. It was pointless keeping it on anyway as she'd only gone there to sleep. At least this way she was on hand if there was a problem.

A new woman had started as a greeter and flirter. Nice enough girl, if a bit dim, but she got the job done and the punters seemed to like her childish innocence, which to be honest was a bit creepy on their part. She called herself Beauty. Apparently, she'd once been married to a beast but had since kicked him out and found a prince; she even had a small bedroom that she'd turned into a library.

"Nowt queer as folk," Widow muttered and shut the curtains across the back door and the kitchen window.

She got on with tidying the reception room, not that it ever got dirty, but a few magazines weren't in the correct piles. She plumped the cushions on the sofa and chairs, then remembered she'd just wasted her time because the renovations were starting in a few hours at nine a.m. The furniture was all getting thrown out.

She went upstairs to inspect the women's rooms. One of the rules of working here was that they were left clean, the beds stripped, the sheets placed in piles on the floor. Widow picked them up in each room and took them to the laundry chute on the landing. She stuffed them inside, and when the cleaner turned up, she'd bag them, ready to be taken to Lil's Launderette.

Satisfied everything was in order, Widow unlocked the door at the bottom of the stairs that led to her apartment, letting herself in and securing the door behind her. She climbed the stairs, the smell of paint still fresh, the wooden flooring so shiny from its varnish. The eaves had been done in wooden slats, painted white. It was a light and airy space, a sanctuary so different from downstairs, which was all brocade wallpaper in dark colours, something George said was too old-fashioned, gaudy, and, quite frankly, hideous. He'd also sledgehammer suggested that she stopped wearing her Victorian dresses, complete with the bustle at the back. He said it gave him the creeps, like she was some strange ghost floating around the place. It had always been her costume at her previous workplace, something she'd worn when she'd been a sex worker, but she conceded that perhaps she needed to let go of the past and usher in the future.

In more ways than one.

The work due to be done would hopefully be completed inside twenty-four hours with several crews coming in. The twins were paying everyone their missed wages. Widow planned to stay up in her lovely attic apartment and read with earplugs in so she didn't hear the banging.

She changed ready for bed, and just as she was about to climb under the covers, the doorbell rang. She glanced at the clock—five a.m.—so it could be the cleaner arriving early, although she ought to be using her key. Then her stomach rolled over. Had she remembered to tell *him* not to turn up this week? She hadn't wanted him anywhere near this place while it was being done up because the twins might be around overseeing things. She should have known he'd have ignored her. A druggie never cared whether they affected your life so long as they got the money for their fix.

She left her apartment and went into one of the front bedrooms downstairs, craning her neck to look down at the door. There he stood, hands in his pockets, his body flicking this way and that because he needed a hit. She should turn him away, she shouldn't give him money, it only encouraged him. He was trouble with a capital T and if he knew exactly how much she earned while here and how much money was on the property at any given time, he'd be robbing it without a second thought.

She'd been putting it off for long enough. It was time—*again*—to tell him he had to stand on his own two feet. Could she do it? Could she completely cut off her emotions and say what had to be said, even if he arrived here with his desperation clawing at him from the inside out?

She went downstairs and opened the front door, gesturing him in and leading him into her office where she had her own private safe. She opened it, shielding the keypad on the door so he couldn't see what she was doing, and reached in to take out the already prepared envelope.

There must be no more envelopes.

She closed the safe and turned to him. "How have you been, son?"

He stared at the envelope. After all, that was the only reason he was here. He didn't come to see her. He didn't give two shits about his 'slag of a mother', but he was fine about taking her money.

"All right," he said.

She passed it to him. "I told you not to come today. I let you know workers would be here soon because the place is getting a makeover. I can't risk the twins seeing you here. This is my job, I don't want to jeopardise it."

"You don't want *me* to, you mean. I've always been a problem to you. You've never wanted me around."

"I haven't wanted you around since you've been injecting shit and sniffing stuff up your nose, no. You're an absolute nightmare when you're high."

He looked in the envelope. "That's not enough."

She raised her eyebrows at the ungrateful fucker. "Excuse me?"

"I owe some cunt money."

"Again?" She sighed, wanting to scream. It was like all the chats she'd had with him regarding this had fallen out of his head. "We've talked about this. That is not my problem. If you owe someone a lot for drugs, you'll have to work out some other way to get the cash. Like find a job?"

He whipped a knife out so quickly it took a moment for her to catch up with his movement. He pointed it at her.

He trembled. "Give me more money or I'll stab you. I swear to God, Mum, don't test me."

She stood her ground, staring him straight in the eye and possibly making the biggest mistake of her life. "No."

His fingers tightened around the handle, and she stared, waiting for the blade to end her life.

To be continued in *Rebury*
Book 35 in the Cardigan Estate

Printed in Great Britain
by Amazon